This is How a Villain is Made

A Novella

Amanda Headlee

Uncomfortably Dark Horror

Book Cover by Don Noble of Rooster Republic

Edited & formatted by 360 Editing, a division of Uncomfortably Dark Horror.

Editor: Candace Nola

Published by Uncomfortably Dark Horror, owned and operated by Candace Nola. Pittsburgh, PA

Follow us on all social media, our Patreon, or on our website to stay up to date on new releases, appearances, and more!

Committed to *"bringing you the best in horror, one uncomfortably dark page at a time."*

Patreon

Website

Contents

OTHER WORKS BY AMANDA HEADLEE

Till We Become Monsters
Madness and Greatness Can Share the Same Face

shows us that though we fear the villain, we should loathe the circumstances that made th em."–Somer Canon, author of *You're Mine*

"*A visceral autopsy of the darkness that creates infamy. Headlee dissects villainy to create an icon.*"–LCW Allingham, Author of *Muse*

"*Amanda Headlee's THIS IS HOW A VILLAIN IS MADE is a must-read for fans of western horror. At the center is Bea, a woman unraveling not because she's weak or sinful but because the men around her weaponize their authority and call it protection. The real frontier in this novella isn't land, it's the brutal truth women carry when they stop pretending men have the answers. Chilling, feminist, and razor-sharp, THIS IS HOW A VILLAIN IS MADE drags you through a bloody descent and leaves you with an ending that's as cathartic as it is just.*"– Nicole M. Wolverton, author of A *Misfortune of Lake Monsters*

DEDICATION

For those who let the fire in—not just to burn, but to become.

Chapter 1

The Morning After

The panicked shock of sensing she isn't alone jolts Bea from her sleep. Her heart flutters as she sits upright in bed, clutching the quilt to her chest, and looks around the sparsely furnished room. After a third cursory look around the room, a smile washes over Bea's frightened face in relief that she is indeed alone and safe. The adrenaline from her reaction gradually subsides in her veins, easing the trauma of days gone by.

The door to the bedroom stands closed, just as she had left it the night before. Bea pushes the patchwork quilt off her body. Sunlight filters through the hand-woven curtains adorning the bedroom windows, casting delicate patterns of light onto the floor. The warmth of the sun radiates into her feet as she walks over to the wooden chair in the corner of the room by the windows. A hastily discarded pair of pants rests on the seatback. Slipping in one leg at a time, she pulls the pants up over her waist and tucks the length of the off-white cotton button-up shirt she'd slept in into the waistband. Both pieces of clothing are a tad too big for her, but she resolves the situation by finding a belt in the dresser on the opposite side of the room. It will be nice to wear a belt. Over the past several months—maybe years—she has spent a lot of time without a belt, hiking up her slacks as they slip to drift off her hips.

The bedroom, despite its barren decor, is cozy. It is a simple space and not overwhelming. A trundle bed with a sagging mattress is draped with an old patchwork quilt that holds an undocumented history. A lone chair holds the clothes Bea wore the day before. A dresser stands against the wall near the open door, opposite the two windows that overlook the vast prairie.

Three of the four dresser drawers house clothing for a man. The top drawer is where she found the belt and other trinkets. When she first opened the drawer and saw the variety of items—jewelry, hairpins, change purses, and other feminine mementos—Bea averted her gaze and, in doing so, noticed a belt coiled on the right side of the drawer. She hastily grabbed the leather strap and slammed the drawer shut, leaving the other contents to address later.

Once dressed, Bea opens the bedroom door and savors stepping over the threshold to the landing at the top of the stairs. She avoids looking at the section of the loft blocked off by a white linen sheet and enjoys the sensation of her eyes crinkling as a smile stretches across her face with each step down the stairs. With a quick comb of her fingers through her wildly curly brown hair—to make herself presentable—Bea reaches the first floor. She steps forward to the front door and opens it.

A warm breeze wraps around her as she steps out onto the porch. Gazing across the prairie, a beautiful new day unfolds panoramically before her, surrounded by an expansive sea of grass, with the remnants of a fading mining town just beyond the grassy swells. The Rockies reach toward the heavens, shrouded in haze as they frame Yellow Creek City.

The smell of the earth and grass fills her nostrils as she inhales a deep breath of fresh, free air. She shakes herself and exhales the breath of the prairie with a whoosh. It's time to start this new day.

As Bea reenters the house, she moves toward the small room on the right, named "the Library" because of the packed bookshelves lining the walls, and sees Emily sitting in the rocking chair in the far corner. The rocking chair dips forward and back ever so slightly as the breeze flows in through the open window beside the chair. Bea wants to believe it is Emily who moves the chair, but she knows her friend no longer has the strength to do so on her own.

Bea's smile fades as she kneels by Emily's side, her back turned to the hallway that runs alongside the stairs leading to the office—an addition—at the back of the house.

"Shall we have our tea outside this morning?" Bea asks, smoothing the apron covering Emily's torso and thighs, hoping her friend wasn't cold in this chair overnight. The only other blanket in the house is in the closet at the back of the office, but Bea isn't ready to go in there to retrieve it. Bea selfishly kept the only available blanket for herself upstairs on the bed. Emily didn't argue. Besides, it turned out to be a warm night.

Bea adjusts the knots of the old dish towel she brought in from the kitchen last night and strung it up between the front two legs of Emily's rocking chair. After confirming that the knots hold firm, Bea gently lifts Emily's right foot and maneuvers it into the dish towel hammock. She carefully does the same with Emily's left foot. Bea caresses the smooth, youthful skin of Emily's cold feet. Both appendages regain some flexibility, but they still exhibit a peculiar soft stiffness.

Once satisfied that both of her friend's feet are securely tucked away, Bea stands. Emily hasn't made a single movement or spoken a word since Bea entered the room. In fact, Emily hasn't uttered a word since...

Bea shakes her head, unable to dislodge the lump in her throat as she focuses on the friend before her, pushing away sour memories of others. Emily's all she has now, and Bea is determined to take care of her friend forever. She runs a hand through Emily's tangled black hair, making a mental note to find a brush later. Bea softly caresses Emily's cheek with a finger. There isn't even a flutter in her friend's cloudy eyes as they stare blankly ahead, never once searching for Bea.

The lump grows larger in her throat. It won't be long until she loses her friend. Emily's body is failing long before it was supposed to.

"Let me see to that tea. But first." Bea grabs the arms of the chair beneath Emily's clawed hands and pulls the rocking chair forward. Once there is enough space between the back of the chair and the corner behind it, Bea slips in and wraps her hands around the top of the chair, her knuckles resting on either side of Emily's head. She gently tilts the chair back on its rungs and slides it toward the front door.

The rungs hit hard against the threshold, and both Bea and Emily tip forward from the force of the stop. If Bea didn't have her knuckles against Emily's skull, she might have tipped her dear friend out of the chair, shattering her fragile body onto the wooden porch floorboards.

"Sorry!" Bea gasps as she tips the chair back, cradling Emily's body between the chair's back and seat. She heaves again, and this time, the rungs of the chair easily clear the threshold. Once outside on the porch, Bea places her friend just to the left of the door. Next to Emily stands a small side table, large enough for two cups of tea, and just beyond that, before the edge of the porch, is another rocking chair—smaller and wobblier than the one Emily sits in. The other chair has likely witnessed quite a bit during its time sitting outside year-round in the Colorado weather.

Emily's chair is much more ornate, with a glossy finish on the amber-colored wood. Its design made Bea wonder if it was imported from the East Coast; it reminded her of the chair her mother used to sit in as she protectively watched Bea play in the yard from the comfort of the front porch of Bea's childhood home.

The chair's arms, rungs, and legs were shaved smooth with a luster that sealed the wood beneath its shine. The seat has a slight divot in the center, and the back features five thin spindles that support the headrest. Bea hopes Emily is comfortable in the chair. If only Emily would say so— just a single word to reassure Bea that everything is okay—and will always be okay.

"I'll be back," Bea says and pats the top of Emily's hand. Her skin is drying out. Bea needs to think about how to address that, as she wants to make Emily as happy as possible.

Walking into the house, Bea still can't dislodge the lump welling in her throat. It feels like a bird rattling in a cage, yearning to escape. Bea refuses to cry; she won't let the tears flow. There's been enough sorrow already. Now, she and Emily are free; there's no reason for sadness.

Entering the kitchen, Bea's mind whirls with thoughts about how she could transform the sparsely decorated rooms of this house into a true home for her and Emily, which surprises her; ever since her arrival, she had wanted nothing more than to leave and move on. Now, she notices the enamel white sink and how it sharply contrasts with the dingy floral off-white wallpaper on the plastered walls, where it bubbles at the seams. In one patch in the upper right corner of the kitchen, the paper has begun to peel away.

She can fix it. She can make this place her own—a home instead of a prison.

In the sink sits an old metal bucket. Its thin handle screeches when Bea lifts it, eliciting a flinch from her. She chides herself, remembering that she's safe now.

She takes the bucket out the front door, past Emily in the rocking chair swaying with the breeze, toward the water pump about fifty feet from the kitchen side of the house. The old iron pump appears orange-red, giving the impression of being painted, but it is actually rusty. The worn handle lets loose its usual screech when pumped, sounding like an old chicken having its neck wrung. A grayish liquid spurts from the nozzle as Bea pumps the handle. Allowing the tainted water to cycle through, she hooks the bucket's handle over the spigot once it runs clear and fills the bucket with the crystal water.

Only a little bit of water is needed for the tea. The rest she will save to drink throughout the day and use for dinner (which she hasn't even begun to plan yet). There isn't much food in the house, and Bea needs to figure out soon what she'll do for Emily and herself. She didn't survive all this time just to die from starvation.

As she pumps the water, her mind drifts to the items in the top drawer of the bedroom dresser, specifically the coin purses. She didn't touch them, but perhaps she should see what is inside each one. Maybe tomorrow. Her stomach clenches as she thinks about the possibility of money. Money that she, herself, didn't earn.

Small waves of water splash against the bucket's rim, and Bea stops pumping. Lifting the bucket off the spigot, she counterbalances the weight of the water in her right hand by extending her left arm straight out to the side. She hisses as the bucket's handle digs into her palm and hurriedly shuffles back toward the house, sloshing water out of the bucket with every few steps.

Drips follow her up the steps, across the porch, and into the house as she makes her way back to the kitchen. Lifting the bucket with both hands, she places it in the sink and then uses a ladle to dip water into the tea kettle on the stove.

When she opens the stove's large belly, all she finds is ash and cinders. It clearly needs cleaning. She clicks her tongue at the dirt inside, but Bea cannot be bothered with that right now. Next to the stove are five logs of wood and some tinder. She retrieves matches from the kitchen hutch.

Stacking the wood inside the stove, she tucks tinder into the gaps and lights it. The tinder catches the flame, drawing it deeper into the stack. Bea holds her breath as she prays for the wood to ignite. It's been a while since she last lit a fire in this stove, and the wood seems dry enough.

With a crackling pop, a flame shoots up between two pieces of wood and crawls across the peeling bark. Bea smiles. She's done it. But this is all the wood available. She bites her lip, pushing aside the nagging thought that to get more, she'll have to go into town.

As the fire burns beneath the kettle, Bea takes two white teacups from the hutch. Delicate pansies adorn the exterior of the cups in shades of purple, yellow, black, and green. She traces the flowers on one cup with the tip of her finger, knowing this will bring Emily joy. Bea sets them on the table and retrieves the tin of tea leaves along with the small tea leaf strainer. Popping open the tin's lid, she feels relieved to find it half full of dried tea leaves.

The kettle whistles sharply, causing Bea to nearly drop the tin. She pats her chest to calm her racing heart, exhaling as she places the tin on the table next to the two cups, then clasps her trembling hands together before reaching for it. The whistle fades when she lifts the kettle from the stovetop. After setting the kettle aside for a moment, Bea puts the tea leaf strainer in one cup, along with a scoop of tea leaves. She picks up the kettle and pours the water into the cup, rehydrating the leaves. Once the tea colors the water, she moves the strainer to the other cup, adds a few more dried tea leaves, and fills the cup in the same way.

The hutch reveals the sugar jar in its usual spot, but it's almost empty. She adds a cube to each cup—deciding they both deserve a little sweetness—leaving her with three cubes in the jar.

Bea returns to the porch to join Emily, holding a teacup in each hand, and sets them on the table between their rocking chairs. Before returning to her chair, Bea delicately brushes her fingertips against the back of Emily's nearest hand. There is no response. The sigh that escapes Bea's lips is heavy with sadness, and she takes a seat in her chair, gently rocking it back and forth to ease the weight resting like a rock in her chest. Birdsong and the rustle of grass create beautiful music that prompts Bea to close her eyes and let herself be consumed by the symphony. Gradually, the weight inside her lifts.

A distant scream shatters the music, followed by shouting. Bea opens her eyes and glances toward the hillcrest that separates this house from the nearby town about a mile away. The right corner of her lip curls toward her eye, and she fully settles back into her chair, increasing the rhythm of her rocking.

"Guessing someone found that message I left on the boarding house's stoop. They'll come looking for the doctor," Bea says.

The hollering fades, returning the two women to the sounds of the prairie, where the breeze creates waves of golden-green ripples across the grass. The lush sound evokes memories of trips to Cape May and Atlantic beaches that Bea enjoyed with her mother during her childhood in the late 1860s. They would sit quietly on blankets atop the sand, surrounded by grassy dunes, the fabric of their dresses flowing around them like islands in the sea. Those days filled Bea with immense happiness, and she cherishes those memories even nearly fifteen years later. Her time with her mother was her only source of joy until her friendship with Emily blossomed. Bea gazes affectionately at Emily, who continues to stare blankly ahead. The wave of happiness fades, and the heaviness in her chest returns. She very well may lose Emily today.

The screams come again, high-pitched—a cry of agony from another woman. Bea focuses on the sounds of panic and calamity to distract herself from thinking about how this day could end.

"I reckon by those screams, the law will be here soon. Been a long time since I last encountered *that* man." The rocking chair softly creaks against the floorboards as Bea recalls the first time she met the town sheriff, "A very long time indeed."

Chapter 2

TRANSACTIONS

THE PATH TO SURVIVAL sometimes leads down a road of sin, and Beatrix Beaumont intended to survive by any means necessary—even if she hadn't originally planned to sell herself to make ends meet. The opportunity presented itself when she arrived in Chicago with fifty dollars in her coin purse—far too little to get her all the way to San Francisco and still have money left for emergencies. The train fare to San Francisco was nearly seventy dollars alone, not including meals. And planning for emergencies was essential, as they could arise at any moment—much like her current predicament, a result of a delayed train from Philadelphia that caused her to miss her transfer. Now stuck in the city overnight, waiting for the next train to Omaha, she needed a way to cover the costs of food and lodging.

She had acquiesced to a request from an affluent-looking man who descended the front steps of his city home clad in a light tweed, knee-length coat. He did not appear to be in a hurry, and when Bea approached him to inquire about job opportunities in his household, he paused for a moment before inviting her inside. The man seemed kind enough, though there was a look in his eyes that a more experienced Bea would have known to steer clear of. Newly on the run, Bea was naïve and uncertain about the world, so when the man led her to his bedroom and asked her how much, she assumed he wanted the second floor of his house cleaned. "How much?" he asked.

"Um, is five dollars reasonable?" she stammered, unsure of typical housekeeping rates but painfully aware that the amount was a lot to ask. She needed the money badly enough to risk sounding foolish. Her hands trembled slightly; she couldn't afford to ask for less.

"Perfectly." His broad, white teeth shone through his smile as he removed his jacket, hung it on the back of a chair, and pulled a miser's purse out of his pocket. Bea started to untie her bonnet, so that she didn't have it flopping in her face as she scrubbed away.

"No, no. Leave that on." His smile widened as he looked at her body from the hem of her dress all the way up to her head.

A shiver ran down her spine when she let go of her bonnet's ribbon and reached for the gold coin he held out before her, pinched between the index finger and thumb of his right hand. When her fingers touched the coin, he seized her by the wrist.

In that chilling moment, it struck Bea with terrifying clarity what was about to unfold. She instinctively recoiled, yanking the coin from his grasp with a sense of foreboding. The man's expression crumbled, a flicker of panic igniting in his dark, haunting eyes as shadows danced around them.

"I'll... I'll double it," he stammered, licking his lips in what Bea took as an effort to entice her further. It worked. The thought of having enough money to continue her escape from Philadelphia weighed heavily in favor of the decision to do whatever was necessary to ensure her survival, even if that meant going somewhere she had never desired.

The secret is to keep breathing, she thought as she inhaled deeply, clutching the gold coin in her hand and dropping her arm to her side. The cool weight of the coin pressed against the soft skin of her palm, absorbing her focus from the reality of the decision she had just made.

The secret is to keep breathing.

After he finished with her, he hastily redressed, muttering a breathless thank you before bolting from the room. Bea recoiled, her senses overwhelmed as the volume and weight of the silence shattered around her. Her body moved of its own accord, trembling as she struggled to rearrange her undergarments and dress. Just as she steadied herself with a hand on the cold foot rail of his bed, he reentered the room, wild-eyed and frantically raking a hand through his disheveled hair. With darting eyes, he thrust a note toward her. Bea's fingers shook violently as she accepted the crisp paper, the elaborate black design stark against the pale linen color. The red stamped seals marred the artwork, an ominous blemish on the already tainted five-dollar note; it felt like a dark omen, whispering of secrets yet to unravel.

"If you are around town for a while, you can come back." He smiled softly. "I'll increase the payment."

Bea forced herself to return the smile. A million thoughts whirled through her mind, with two-thirds of those thoughts echoing a powerful urge to vomit and cry. Meanwhile, the remaining third pondered his offer. More money could get her all the way to San Francisco without having to stop in every few cities to figure out how to afford the rest of the trip.

She never returned to him, but that incident taught her about a new realm in the world, one she hated and feared. Yet, at the same time, she realized how she could exploit it to survive. Thus, whenever she needed money to continue her travels west, she used her resources to support her endeavors. How she wished she could turn a blind eye to the sin she was committing. But she had no other choice. She needed to survive. God should understand that, she hoped.

This level of survival was not without its risks. A more mature Bea would ultimately take pride in her wit; however, this version of Bea, despite her experience with people—particularly men—was still in the process of development, which sometimes put her safety at risk. Alone on a bench at the Yellow Creek City train platform during a warm, waning Colorado afternoon, Bea pondered whether this was one of those instances.

A man approached, wearing dark brown pants with a matching vest covering a dirty white shirt. Around his waist was a leather gun belt with straps filled with bullets. The fact that Bea couldn't see his eyes as he shielded them with a hand against the rays of the setting sun unnerved her the most. Eyes were windows to the soul, and she could tell a lot about someone just by looking at them. Six harsh months on the run had taught her that.

As she tried to make eye contact, the flash of gold on his chest caused her to immediately drop her gaze and hide behind the brim of her bonnet. A *sheriff*. She slid her dusky floral-patterned carpet bag a few inches away from her side on the worn wooden bench, leaving no room for anyone to sit close.

Her mind raced with reasons why this lawman was appearing on the train platform. His stride was long and purposeful—he had business here. The only other person besides Bea was a man who lay sound asleep next to his travel trunk on the platform floor. She breathed in and exhaled a prayer that the sheriff was here for the sleeping man. Bea's fingers twitched at the thought that she might have been found, and her father sent the lawman here to collect her. She lowered her head, hoping it would somehow make her invisible. She tried to calm her racing heart by first focusing on the dusty floorboards, then on the late-afternoon heat, and finally on the little beads of sweat prickling her neck that rolled beneath her dress collar and trailed down her spine.

The secret is to keep breathing, she thought, reciting a mantra that helped calm her and keep her present.

"You travelin' alone?" The voice came before the fancy gold-tipped boots stepped into her field of vision beneath her bonnet. If she didn't acknowledge him, who knew how he'd react? She looked up at the sheriff, trying to replace the fear etched on her face with a look of calmness and innocence.

"Naw. My Daddy's waitin' for me in Denver City, and we're heading home to San Francisco. I'm coming from Yuma after caring for a sick aunt." The lie rolled effortlessly off her tongue—one she'd well-rehearsed as she walked along the dusty road to Yellow Creek City. She hoped that if this man was an agent of her father, saying her 'Daddy' was waiting in Denver City, might convince the sheriff that he had the wrong girl. And if the sheriff wasn't sent by her father, he'd know she had someone waiting for her who was expecting her arrival.

He looked her over and smiled before saying, "You look to be a woman of class. Not safe to be traveling out there on the roads alone. Why not just take the train from Yuma?"

"I missed that one. My aunt suggested I take a coach here to catch the evening train." The latter was not entirely a lie. Bea had come to Yuma quite by accident. After arriving in Omaha from Chicago, she was supposed to change trains in Cheyenne but accidentally boarded the wrong train and found herself in Kansas City. Once she was back on a train heading in the right direction, anxiety surged within her; she felt grateful to have avoided any encounters with the men her father likely sent to track her down. Panic grew from her anxiety as the train headed toward Denver City. When the train stopped in Yuma, she quietly disembarked and hired a stagecoach to Greenly, where she intended to catch a new train heading north to Cheyenne—completely bypassing Denver City. Something deep inside her urged her to keep her distance from Denver City.

Unfortunately, the stagecoach broke down just three miles from Yellow Creek City, leading her to yet another unexpected detour. Now, her only option was to take a train from this point—a journey that held the risk of arriving in Denver City, where she could potentially run into her father's men if they were still on the lookout for her. Denver City was the next largest city along her route. With each step towards Yellow Creek City, the unease in her stomach grew stronger.

"Ah, that's a shame. And I hope your auntie is feeling better," he said.

Bea nodded, still unsure if the Sheriff was with her father or not.

"Though I have bad news. Came here to tell you folks that tonight's train is canceled. It ran into a herd of cows before Fort Morgan. The telegraph operator says the morning train is on schedule, so you'll have to catch that one. You can exchange your ticket with Mitchell before the train gets here in the morning." He nodded toward the empty ticket booth before running a hand through his thick, graying hair. He had a nicely chiseled face with a shadow of a beard. His eyes were bright and sharp.

Bea exhaled a slow sigh of relief. He wasn't here for her. He wasn't sent here by her father. He'd just come to deliver some particularly bad news. However, despite his kind demeanor, something felt off. Perhaps it was his crooked smile. But it was something she had to push aside because she was in a tough situation, with nowhere to stay. After her costly mistake of boarding the wrong train to Kansas City and the stagecoach fare that got her this far, she lacked enough funds to reach San Francisco. She couldn't afford to risk what little she had left after buying a ticket to Denver City on an unplanned room expense for the night.

The stagecoach breaking down was an unplanned hindrance, but this... she looked around the platform, then at the small town behind her. Open prairie grasslands surrounded the town, with nothing else between there and the small hills rolling toward the towering Rockies on the horizon. Bea glanced down at the bench, pondering whether it was safe enough for her to sleep on for the night. Sleeping under the stars in a town she knew nothing about terrified her more than the thought of arriving in Denver City and potentially falling into the waiting hands of her father's men.

Bea wanted to keep on the run until she reached San Francisco, where she could disappear into the big city—maybe start over, find a respectable husband, and live a quiet life raising a family. A husband would mean safety. Protection.

She hadn't been captured yet, but deep down, she knew her father was still searching for her. Heading west was the only way to evade his grasp; a lesson she had learned the hard way. Following her initial escape to Pittsburgh, where she fled with two hundred dollars in bank notes and coins stolen from her father's office safe, she rented a room and managed on her own for several months, only to be found at last by a man her father had sent to bring her back. That was when she realized she needed to put as much distance as possible between herself and her father.

Tears pricked her eyes at the thought of being trapped. She needed money, and fast. Bea looked at the sheriff, who had a half-cocked eyebrow as he returned her gaze. She knew he didn't immediately take her to be a woman who sold herself. She did well to hide that. Growing up in Philadelphia, she'd been a young lady of high society, so she maintained that appearance as best as she could during her travels. She carried three of her prettiest dresses in her bag, which didn't make her stand out in a crowd but allowed her to still seem like she lived that high-society lifestyle.

Today, she wore a soft yellow ribbed silk dress with embroidered cutwork trim that looked as fresh and bright as the morning sun, despite being worn on the run. The bodice fit perfectly to showcase how she had grown into adulthood—without the support of a mother.

This dress was, in fact, her mother's. In one of her favorite memories, Bea watched her mother delicately select the buttons to be sewn onto the bodice at the dressmaker's shop. She remembered her mother running her fingers over the lace of the overskirt hem and the bodice sleeve cuffs. Of all the dresses her mother owned, this was her favorite.

It was the same dress she had worn when she encountered the man in Chicago and continued to wear—albeit uncomfortably hiked up—through that first experience that showed her men seemed to prefer women of a high-standing nature over a woman they could find at a brothel. Thus, it was easy to make money, especially as she traveled from town to town since she didn't have to see the same man twice.

Bea pushed the memories of that first act she had performed in her mother's dress into the darkest corners of her mind. The sheriff would have to suffice in this instance. Bea tipped her head back, allowing her bonnet to slide off, revealing soft, rich, brown curls.

"Well, I don't quite know what I'll do with myself now." She smiled and batted her eyes.

His face flushed red, and he looked around. The only person in their vicinity was the sleeping man. "How about you come back with me to the jailhouse, and we'll figure out what you can do?"

Bea breathed in sharply.

"No, no, just to get out of the sun to talk and get you a glass of water. I wouldn't be able to live with myself if I let a woman like you sleep out here for the night," he said.

"What about him?" she asked, nodding toward the other man.

"Eh, that's just Jessup Birch. He's a local. Headin' to Denver City to see his ma." He walked over and kicked the sleeping man in the foot, causing a plume of dust to rise off the dirty train platform floorboards. "Wake up, ya drunk."

Jessup sat up quickly with a snort. "I ain't do nothin' this time, Dodson." Jessup's arms shot up over his head, hands trembling in the sheriff's presence.

"Trains late. Git home. It'll be here in the morning," the sheriff said.

"Oh." The man let out a long sigh of relief. "Thought I'd gone and done somethin' stupid again."

The sheriff stepped back, not offering one hand to help the man up. Jessup groaned as he climbed to his knees. He brushed off the front of his pants and shirt, loosening any dirt that had settled on him. He had been there before Bea arrived, so she had no idea how long he'd been waiting. Jessup looked at her as he stood tall. She grew cold when their eyes met—a cloud of negative energy seemed to surround the man. She quickly looked away.

"Ma'am." Jessup's smile crept slowly across his face, exposing several missing teeth. His eyes brightened as he assessed her from head to heeled boots. "My, my, what do we have here?" He swept a hand through his thinning hair.

Bea's stomach churned.

"Alright, Jessup, get outta' here." The sheriff crossed his arms and glared at the man.

"I'm going, I'm going." The man chuckled, then dragged his trunk off the platform and across the dusty road toward the right side of town.

Relief washed over Bea. She said nothing about the man but asked, "The train being delayed because of cows is a regular occurrence?"

"This train being delayed happens often. Come on." The sheriff turned and walked across the platform, then down the steps to the dusty road.

Bea followed, lugging her bag. He didn't offer to carry it for her.

"I'm Dodson, by the way," he said to her, not turning to look.

"Bea," she replied, not wanting to offer more information about herself. He seemed satisfied with that before he broke into a rambling—and uninvited—overview of the town's history.

T HE HEAT OF THE setting prairie sun wasn't as oppressive as it had been earlier in the day, but the damp sweat under Bea's armpits and lower back made her even more uncomfortable in the sheriff's company. It seemed like it hadn't rained in days. Swirls of dust kicked up as they walked the lonely road through the center of town. A pang of feeling lost coiled in her stomach as she took in the town's emptiness. Being out west was vastly different from growing up among paved streets and brick buildings. The nature around here starkly contrasted her family's small summer home nestled among the tall trees of the Pennsylvania forests outside of Philadelphia.

Bea felt exposed in this little town on the open grasslands. God had a clear line of sight on her, and there was nowhere to hide. She shifted the weight of the bag in her hands and sighed.

"Town's nearly dried up," Dodson said as they walked through the heart of the town. Ramshackle buildings stood dusty and tall in the setting sun. A tinge of tiredness painted across the town's visage and landscape. "My daddy moved me to these parts in '59, during the gold rush. It was just me and him, as Mama had died of consumption a few years earlier. I often helped him pan for gold in the creek. That's just north of here. Yellow Creek." He looked at Bea and smiled. "Reason why this is Yellow Creek City."

"A unique name," Bea said with a light voice and a smile to disguise her sarcasm.

The sheriff didn't take notice. "You know why the creek is called Yellow Creek?" Bea had a good feeling as to why but humored him with a shake of her head. "It's because of all the gold found there."

She faked a laugh and shook her curls before giving him her sweetest smile. Her flirtatious tactics worked as he walked a bit closer to her. "I can imagine what the town looked like in its prime."

"This was a busy place back then—almost three hundred people at one point. A few houses are occupied outside this main stretch further out in the prairie, but most of the abandoned houses have been taken down. Used the material elsewhere."

Bea wondered how a town like this could survive with no local economy apart from a dust-covered saloon, The Claim, which stood near the center of town.

Dodson continued, "There're less than a hundred people here now. But we at least have a doctor. Lives way out beyond the town's limits. Only makes house calls, as he likes his solitude. I'm the one tasked to fetch him during emergencies. But we at least have one when in need."

"Will you ever leave here?" she asked.

"Nah. A place like this, it's in my bones."

"Sheriff!" A woman wearing a tight and ill-fitting black dress sauntered out of a building to their right. "There you are, sweetie."

"What do you want now?" he growled at the woman.

"Now, Sheriff." she winked at him. "Don't you be all gruff with me."

Sheriff Dodson stood straighter and held out a hand, beckoning her to continue.

"Now you know I am missing two girls. Where are they?" she said, her voice becoming more formal and clipped. Bea held back the smile that tugged at her lips. She liked this woman's authority.

"Maggie, how do you know your girls didn't hightail it out of here? Get whisked away by some charmer."

The woman, Maggie, put her hands on her hips and stepped up to him. While nearly a foot shorter than Sheriff Dodson, Bea had a feeling Maggie could hold her own against him.

"I know my girls, and I treat them well. They would never up and leave without telling me." She jabbed a finger at his chest. "Someone took them. Probably took them from the rooms in my house. Right out from under my nose!"

"Oh, come now, Maggie, no one is abducting women 'round here."

"I tell you, something bad is going on between here and Denver City. You mark my words; this will come back to you, Dodson. So, you better find my girls!" With a final jab to his chest, Maggie turned and returned to the building she'd first sauntered out of.

"Damn, woman," Dodson grumbled and rubbed at his chest where Maggie had poked him.

"What happened?" Bea asked.

Dodson pursed his lips. "Some folks have gone missing here and there." Changing the subject, he pointed toward a building down the road from them, the last one on the left side. "That's my place there. Second floor. Right above the jailhouse. It's nothing fancy, but it's home."

Bea shivered. "Women have gone missing?"

"Nothing for you to worry your little head over. You'll be gone with the train tomorrow, right?" His smile made the hair on the back of her neck stand on end. He hardly made this experience exciting. While he had a handsome face, she struggled to overlook the stains that ringed the armpits of his dirty white shirt. This was a man who didn't take care of himself. Bea knew his kind all too well. They focused solely on themselves because they got whatever they wanted. Bea could tell this because he'd asked her nothing about herself except for what they'd discussed at the train station. Everything else had been about him and this godforsaken town. And now the missing women. She wanted to leave this place as soon as possible.

The thin, single, wood-paneled front door of the jail-house creaked open under Dodson's hand. Sure enough, the interior was just as he described—lackluster. The room's oppressiveness added weight to the hot, stagnant air that fermented within. The heavy taste lodged in the back of Bea's throat. She coughed.

Dodson laughed. "Sorry, a bit dusty in here."

Bea forced a smile as she swallowed hard to wash away the sticky feeling in her mouth and throat. Nothing in the room provided any comfort. A worn wooden desk flanked by a hard, rickety chair made up Dodson's office. The bars separating her from the interior of the jail cell did nothing for the décor except keep her from getting too close to a stained straw mat. A wave of itchiness electrified her scalp as she dared to imagine what bugs lived in the material. Despite the three thinly clad, curtained windows—the two in the front of the building and one behind Dodson's desk—the interior remained dark and dank.

"Like I said, not much here, but it's home. Well, upstairs is. This is just where I work." He walked up a set of stairs that disappeared behind the right wall of the jail cell.

"Kind soul," Bea spat under her breath as she switched her heavy bag from her right hand to her left and shook out her numbing fingers. She had held onto this bag for far too long, and she relished the thought of being able to put it down. Bea walked toward the steps. Dodson was near the top, each step creaking under his weight.

The staircase led into a dusky haze that lacked sunlight. There was just enough ambient light for her to make out the entire staircase and each step. Bea hoisted her skirt in one hand and her bag in the other as she stumbled up the uneven steps. Her shoulders bounced off the stairwell walls due to her struggle to balance her skirt and bag.

Despite the calamity of her ascent and the weight of dread she carried between her shoulder blades, she felt cooler at the top of the stairs. Bea was quite sure he had motives for her, and her courage was ready to ask for payment before they got to work. It would be a transaction, after all.

His living quarters were as sparse as downstairs, but not as stagnant, since he'd left the windows open. Thin white curtains—the same as downstairs—flitted in the breeze. Bea breathed in the cooler air, allowing it to calm her after the exhausting stair climb.

A washstand with an oval mirror stood beside the side window. Between the two street-facing windows rested a table with a single chair. The metal-framed bed, covered with a tattered quilt and a yellowing pillow, leaned against the wall separating the room from the staircase. The only other possible light source in the room—which remained unlit—was a kerosene lamp sitting atop the table.

"So, I might be able to help you with your predicament and get you on your way today without having to spend the night in town." His smile grew dark and unappetizing.

Bea shifted and set her bag down on the floorboards. She needed money and nothing more, yet she humored him all the same. "What do you propose?"

"I have a friend with a wagon that could take you to Denver City. He owes me a favor. You'd be there by midnight. But I'd need something in return." He stepped forward and cupped the curls that hung down the left side of her head before running his fingers through them. A smile of pleasure tugged at the left corner of his mouth. "I never had someone like you before."

"I'd rather have money," she said.

He released her hair and stepped back. Bea knew she had shocked him by not rebuking his offer. A curious darkness crept into his eyes. "You're demanding something of me? I'm the law in this town."

She glanced down at the floorboards and gathered the strength to express her expectations before looking back up at him. "I'm sorry, I'm not demanding. It's just that I'm going to give you something. And I would like something in return."

"Huh." He stepped back and looked down at her with hooded eyes. "Imagine that—a woman with a backbone. Well, I wouldn't say you have a backbone. You're kind of meek there, but you're trying. I can respect that. How much are you wanting?"

A lump rose in her throat, but she forced herself to maintain her stance and look at him. *Don't show him your tears. Tell him what you want.* "One night's room and board at The Claim plus ten dollars."

His eyes widened with anger, igniting fear in Bea's chest. His face flushed as he ran his hand through his greying hair. "That's a lot of money."

In that moment, Bea felt terribly unsafe. She needed to get out of there. Reaching for her bag, she said, "Thank you for letting me know about the train delay. I must be going."

"Wait." He grabbed her wrist. "I'll get you room and board at The Claim, but I'll only give you five dollars. After we're done."

She dropped her bag and wrenched her arm from his grip. "I... No. Ten dollars, plus the room and board. And before we start. Please."

Bea knew she shouldn't be negotiating with him and should take what he offered, but she needed more than that to help fund the remainder of the trip. She had to recoup the money she lost in the mix-up of getting on the wrong train in Omaha. Dodson stared at her for a long minute. Eventually, he nodded. "You're good at standing your ground. Daddy taught you well." He held out a hand for her to shake.

Bea didn't take it. His comment rattled her, and before she could contain herself, the words, "My daddy didn't teach me anything," slipped past her lips.

Dodson stopped smiling. He went to his bed and retrieved a box from underneath it. "Forget you saw this, or you'll find yourself missing." His eyes locked onto hers. "You hear me?"

She swallowed hard and nodded, believing him.

He returned, handing her eleven one-dollar notes. "Buy yourself a drink with your dinner. You're going to need it after I'm through with you." Bea placed the money in the coin purse in her bag, then stood tall and began to undress under the heated gaze of the Yellow Creek City sheriff.

Chapter 3

FEARFUL SYMMETRY

B EA SKIPPED LIGHTLY AS she walked down the dusty road toward The Claim. She had a coin purse full enough to cover her night's room and board, plus her remaining fare west. This took care of her immediate needs, and she pushed aside the growing concern about how she would afford meals for the rest of her journey and any potential emergencies. She needed to concentrate on the present and find a safe place to rest for the night.

Her time with the sheriff had been rough, to say the least. She was grateful that the bruises, which would bloom over the next few hours, would be concealed beneath her dress. Despite her relief at having money, Bea worried about some form of retaliation for asking for so much. This was the first time she truly felt she had pushed a client too far.

In any event, she was quite sure she'd left him passed out on his bed. He shouldn't cause her any trouble tonight. He'd been snoring loudly as she quietly dressed, double-checked the money in her coin purse, and snuck out of the jailhouse without raising him.

Bea pushed open the thin doors to The Claim and a woody, decaying smell enveloped her, as though—just like the jailhouse—the building hadn't experienced fresh air in years.

Empty tables cluttered the saloon—except for one table to her right, occupied by an older couple. Behind them, a mounted black bear stood on its hind legs, its mouth perpetually open in a silent roar, with the fur on its head and shoulders grey with dust. The bar to her left had long shelves lined with partially filled bottles, arranged haphazardly on the wooden planks. She approached the once-opulent but now faded bar, featuring a curved armrest and a smooth surface pockmarked by years of wear and tear. As she passed a man slumped over the bar, his head resting on folded arms and a half-full glass of amber liquid in front of him, he snored loudly, creating the only ambient sound in the entire saloon. The bartender, standing behind the bar drying a glass, barely glanced at her.

"Excuse me?" Bea said, standing in front of the bartender.

He made eye contact before looking her up and down. Despite traveling nonstop for more than six months and fresh from a romp with the town sheriff, Bea looked more put together than the folks of this town.

"Don't get many outsiders here since the boom started to die in the early '60s," the bartender said.

Bea smiled. "Could I rent a room for the night and order dinner?"

"Just a night?" The bartender cocked an eyebrow. "You conducting...business?"

Bea felt her face flush. "No, just passin' through."

"You alone?"

"I'm traveling home for my aunt's funeral. My father will be waiting for me at the Denver City train station tomorrow," she lied.

"Fifty cents for a room and dinner." The bartender held his hand out for payment.

"Could I have a whiskey too?" Bea asked.

He glared at her. "No business in the room. I run a clean place here. Twelve cents for the whiskey." He took her money, went to the register, and returned, slapping a key down on the bar. "Room two."

Bea took the key and made a motion to sit at the bar, but he glared at her once more. She returned the look in kind, grabbed her whiskey, walked to a table beside the bar, and sat down, sliding her bag under the table in front of her. Within the first two months of running away, she had learned to always protect her bag. Having nearly half of her money pickpocketed from this very bag once when she wasn't looking had been a tough but valuable lesson.

It was sheer luck that they had stolen only the money and not the soft brown leather coin purse as well. The coin purse was a gift from her mother for her seventh birthday—just before her mother passed away. Whoever withdrew the cash had broken the button that kept the coin purse closed. She had to replace it with a pin until she could find the appropriate button to fix it.

The whiskey stung her roughly bitten lips and burned down her throat as she swallowed, pushing thoughts of her mother to the back of her mind. Bea loved the feeling of the fire within her chest, a feeling of being alive. She took her time sipping it, hoping to save some to accompany her dinner. The bartender, however, continued to clean his glassware and didn't make any move to get her dinner started.

She had nearly finished her drink when a man entered the saloon and went straight to the bar. He was well-dressed in clean slacks, a white shirt, and a black coat. With slicked-back hair and a fresh-looking face, she noted that there didn't seem to be a speck of dust on him—the complete opposite of Sheriff Dodson. Their eyes met, and Bea shivered. Cold and dark, yet she couldn't look away from him. His face was quite agreeable. Then he started coughing, having to place a hand on the edge of the bar to steady himself.

"Doctor," the bartender grunted and placed a glass of water on the bar.

"Dinner, please," the man said after clearing his throat with a drink of water.

"Yes 'sir. Good evenin' walk to my fine establishment?"

"It was." The man set the glass down and leaned closer to the bartender.

Bea heard him whisper, "Is she alone?"

"Aye," replied the bartender.

"That's not safe. I'll join her for dinner. Put it on my tab."

"Sir," Bea snapped, "I'm quite safe and have already paid for my own dinner." She shifted in her seat, annoyed that he would make such an assumption that she wasn't safe and worried about *why* he thought that.

He raised his finger to the bartender. Without a word, the bartender shuffled over to the cash register, its brass dull and dusty under the dim light. After a moment, he returned and pressed something into the man's hand.

The man walked up to the empty seat in front of her and sat down without asking for permission. "Honestly, ma'am, I'm alone and hungry. Wouldn't mind having someone to talk to while I ate."

She looked at him, unsure.

He slid a dollar coin across the table to Bea. "Good conversation and a meal are all I want."

Bea was unnerved, but he seemed genuine. She had a good sense for reading men. Since she'd left Philadelphia, Bea kept a low profile, rarely speaking to anyone. A pang of loneliness echoed through her. What would it hurt to have dinner with this man? Nothing more would come of it—she'd assure herself that she'd be gone by morning.

"What's your name, stranger?" Bea asked as she picked up the coin, accepting the man's offer to cover her meal. What he returned to her exceeded the cost of her meal, whiskey, and room—and she chose not to say anything.

"Jonatan. And yours?"

"Bea."

"Nice to meet you, Bea." He extended his hand, and she reciprocated the handshake.

"It is nice to meet you too, Johnathan."

A shadow passed over his eyes as he pursed his lips. "Jonatan. It's Jon-a-tan."

Bea gasped. "I'm so sorry! Jonatan." She smiled, trying to calm his anger. "That is a lovely sounding name. I'm not sure I've heard it before."

The shadow lifted from his face, and Jonatan sat back tall in his seat, a smile pulled tightly across his lips. "My family immigrated from Scandinavia. The name is my lineage."

"How lovely to have such history passed down to you. May I assume your father is named the same?"

Jonatan chuckled. "He is of the same. Or more, I am of the same as he. Why, in 1759, my great-grandfather..."

Bea forced a smile and suppressed the tension in her chest caused by Jonatan's reaction. She maintained a look of apt attention firmly on her face as Jonatan chattered on about his family ancestry. Over the years, she had become quite skilled at feigning interest.

T HEIR VENISON AND BOILED potatoes dinner was cold before they took their first bite—not because it had arrived that way, but because they'd talked non-stop. Bea found herself captivated by Jonatan's stories of growing up in New York, including visits to museums, the library, and the park. While her mother was alive, she had similar experiences in Philadelphia—but she said nothing about herself to him. She loved hearing about his favorite painters and authors, and she responded in kind.

"I'm quite enamored by the work of William Blake," he said as he cut his venison.

"*The Tyger* and *The Lamb* are two of my favorite poems," she replied.

Jonatan put his utensils down and cocked an eyebrow at her. "You aren't from around here if you know of Blake's work."

She dabbed her mouth with her napkin. "I grew up in Philadelphia."

"You had a cultured upbringing as well?"

"Yes."

He seemed to sense she wouldn't offer any more information, so he returned to Blake. "What is it about those two specific poems that you like?"

"The duality between the darkness and light. That our Lord created these two binary opposites on the same planet. And that they were intentionally created to coexist here."

Jonatan snorted. "I hardly agree. When we analyzed the poems in my university literature class, we were told it was about the industrialization of our great cities encroaching on the natural landscape."

Bea thought for a moment. "I could see that as a possibility for the rhetoric of the poems. But to me, it represents God's creation of the light and darkness on Earth, building both with a purpose."

"And where did you learn that?"

"My mother first introduced me to the poems." She smiled warmly at the memory. "We'd sit up late into the night in my bedroom reading and talking about what they meant."

"So, you were not trained by a scholar?"

Heat burned in her cheeks as she bowed her head, hiding her embarrassment. She'd only attended school at a young age to learn basic English and arithmetic skills. Everything else she learned from her mother. After her mother died, Bea was forced to stay home and keep the house.

"God did not intentionally create the darkness. Evil is God's enemy, and every day evil tries to dethrone him." His fist landed on the table, causing their tableware to clatter.

Bea flinched and then looked around the saloon. No one else took notice.

"I do disagree." She paused and flinched once more, as if she were waiting for his hand to meet her face, but he didn't react. Just continued to glare at her. She cleared her throat. "But as you said, I was not trained by a scholar."

Jonatan stared at her with cold, dark eyes; his jaw muscles pulsed as he pursed his lips.

"Let's talk about something else." Bea shifted uncomfortably in her seat before taking the conversation in a different direction. "Tell me about your family."

This change in topic—one that focused on him—immediately dissolved his ire, and his face brightened as though the prior conversation never occurred. "My father is a great physician and a devout Christian. He raised me well and pushed me to follow in his footsteps. He also supported my dream of heading out west after graduation to establish my own practice in a town in need of a doctor."

He took a couple of bites of food and then started to cough violently. Bea made a move to help him. He held up a hand and cleared his throat. "Just something that happens from time to time. All's well."

Bea settled and continued the conversation. "He sounds like a good man."

"He is. A very loving man. He bought me an exquisite tortoiseshell bistoury knife for my surgical tool kit as a graduation gift."

Grim, she thought, but smiled anyway. "And what of your mother?"

Jonatan grew silent. His grey eyes darkened once more, and he stared at his plate for several moments. Bea regretted the question and was about to change the subject again when Jonatan stood and left the saloon without a word.

Bea sat in confusion and disbelief. No one took notice of Jonatan's hasty departure.

She picked at her meal for a while but decided she wasn't hungry. It had been a long day. While she enjoyed part of her conversation with Jonatan, he became quite strange toward the end—strange enough to make her uncomfortable. As he sat before her, a stinging sensation radiated through the air between them, making it feel heated. Once he left, a calm coolness enveloped Bea, and relief washed over her. It was a pity because her initial conversation with him had been wonderful and intellectual.

Bea folded her napkin beside her half-eaten meal. She chuckled to herself, reflecting on Jonatan's change in behavior when her interpretation of Blake's poem conflicted with his. His blatant mood swing confirmed in Bea's mind that her analysis of the poems was valid. That was a man who contained both light and dark.

Exhausted after the long, exhausting day, she left the table and took her bag upstairs for the night. Upon reaching her room door, she found it unlocked. Too tired to care, since this seemed to be a safe establishment, she walked over to the nightstand and lit the kerosene lamp. Then, she placed her bag on the bed. As she did, footsteps sounded behind her.

Bea turned.

Jonatan stood behind her, hands clasped together at his waist.

"Jonatan!" Bea said, startled.

"I mean no harm. I just..." He unclasped his hands and held them up, palms toward her. She didn't relax and took a step to the side, away from him.

"What I mean to say—" Jonatan covered his mouth as he broke out into a coughing fit. Bea took a step forward, any fear that she had dissolved. He held up his free hand toward her, indicating to stay put.

"Are you...okay?" she stammered, unsure why she felt any concern for this man who had come uninvited into her space.

He stood upright and tugged down at the collar of his throat before wiping at his vest as though it were covered with dust. He cleared his throat. "I'm fine. As I was saying, I have a proposition for you."

The temperature in the room seemed to have dropped, and Bea shivered. She knew it. There was always a catch. Nothing in life is for free.

"You said I didn't owe you anything for dinner." She narrowed her eyes at him. "And now you're here propositioning me?"

Jonatan's eyes went wide. "My goodness, no! What an abhorrent thing to think!" He scowled at her, and Bea's face flushed with embarrassment.

"I would like it if you'd come work for me. See, I am in need of a housekeeper," he said.

Bea looked at him, puzzled. Following someone to their bedroom was a rather unconventional way to hire them. She wasn't sure if she could trust him.

"I had said that I'm traveling. My father is waiting for me in Denver City," she said.

Jonatan's eyes narrowed before his expression softened. "No, you didn't tell me that. In fact, you kept the reason why you are here in Yellow Creek City to yourself, to which I will not pry. However, I get the sense that you are running away from something rather than running to something, and I would like to offer you some help for the time being."

"What makes you think that I'm running away from something?" Bea stood tall, though she felt uncomfortable with the conversation.

He smiled. "I enjoyed our conversation tonight and would like for it to continue. This is another reason why I am offering you a job. There are not many folks around here who've read Blake, much less any other page of great literature."

As she digested his words, Bea flicked her thumbnails against her index finger. She desperately needed money. What she received from Dodson was enough to complete her trip, but there would be nothing left for her to live on without immediately taking on work—clients—upon her arrival in San Francisco. "What'll the job pay?"

"We can talk about payment another day, to which you will be compensated, but at this very moment, I can offer you a roof over your head and meals, which you'd cook, of course," he said.

Inwardly, she groaned. She hated cooking, but the promise of a roof over her head was tempting, as was the safety of hiding in this town. No one would come looking for her here. She would figure the rest out when the time came; she always does. "What else do I have to do?"

"Just general cleaning. I rarely have patients visit my house as I prefer to make house calls; however, when I do have patients, I like to have a tidy house. I tend not to find the time to clean between seeing patients and my research."

"Research?" she asked.

The stern look returned to his face. "That is something that you won't be privy to, which will make my office off-limits for your duties. I'll maintain the cleanliness there."

Strange, Bea thought, but despite his quirkiness, she hoped that Jonatan was a safe person. He was a doctor, after all. And she could use a stable place to stay for a while, which would also allow her to earn money.

"I accept your proposal." She smiled and held out her hand.

"Very good," he said, walking past her to pick up her things off the bed. Bea looked at him holding her things and nodded, content with her decision.

Chapter 4

FLIGHT OF FANCY

B EA RAKED THE BURNING wood in the cast iron stove, shifting the embers and remaining chunks of log toward the back, leaving only a few embers at the front. This stove had become her greatest nemesis; the water wouldn't boil, and the food always burned because she couldn't regulate the heat properly underneath the stove's two burners. It was a small stove that didn't even have an oven, just one large chamber in which to burn wood. Jonatan said that if she'd ever wanted to bake bread, she'd have to use one of his stoneware bowls and place it in the wood chamber—a feat Bea never risked attempting, knowing full well that, with her skills, the bread would bake into a lump of charcoal.

At her father's home in Philadelphia, they had a gas stove. And the only staff that her father kept on was a cook, as he said that Bea could burn a piece of toast just by looking at it.

However, today, Bea was determined to cook the perfect breakfast by experimenting with the placement of the embers. She had the kettle full of water sitting at the back of the stove and a pan of eggs in the front. Once those were done, she'd scoop some embers forward to increase the heat on the pan to fry up some bacon. The movement of the burning wood pieces sparked, sending flames licking at the top of the wood chamber.

"Success!" Bea said, stirring the eggs to scramble them while watching them firm up without any char. In a few moments, she portioned the eggs into two, scraped them onto the waiting plates on the kitchen table, and then dropped a few rations of bacon into a sizzling pan. The tea kettle whistled, and she poured hot water over the first flowered teacup that held the tea leaves and strainer.

As she left the tea to darken, she flipped the bacon, which was reaching the perfect balance between crispy and chewy. She then moved the tea strainer from the filled cup to the empty one, added more dried tea leaves, and poured in hot water to let it steep. The bacon was done, and she portioned the meat onto the plates alongside the eggs.

The breakfast table was set, and Bea clasped her hands to her chest with glee. She had made the perfect breakfast.

"Jonatan!" she called out as she walked to the library. "Jonatan, breakfast is ready!"

Bea couldn't contain her smile as he walked groggily from the hallway, a notebook grasped in his right hand with a pencil tucked between the pages. His hair was mussed, and his clothes were a bit rumpled. Bea was shocked to see him come from his office instead of his bedroom, given that his bedroom door was closed. She had thought he was upstairs.

He yawned as he walked right past her without a "Good Morning," sat at the table, and dug into the meal. His trusty notebook lay just to the right of his plate. Bea's smile slightly faded, but she attributed his lack of morning formality to exhaustion. He'd just returned from a trip yesterday, and she could hear him working late in the office. Honestly, she wasn't quite sure when he went to sleep. Bea's full smile returned when she sat at the table and dug into her own plate. Everything was perfect. She was so proud.

"Hello and welcome home! I think I have finally mastered this stove of yours." She chirped.

Jonatan chewed and swallowed a sip of tea. "The food is merely average this morning. You still need more work."

Bea flinched at the statement. "Nothing is burnt!" She forced a smile to hide her disappointment at his reaction.

Jonatan mumbled something she couldn't quite hear, pushed his plate to the center of the table, and dragged his notebook in front of him. Unwrapping the leather strap, the book popped open to the pages that held his pencil. His words were already scrawled across the left page, but the right page remained blank as he scratched with his pencil at the top line. Bea couldn't read his handwriting; it was too messy.

He always carried that damn notebook with him, scribbling away but never sharing his thoughts. He often wrote a lot at the kitchen table after they had eaten, while Bea busied herself with the cleanup. Despite not being able to clearly read his handwriting, Jonatan always hovered over the notebook, using his non-dominant arm to block her view. This made Bea feel quite self-conscious because she wondered if he was writing about her.

"What are you writing down in your notebook?" she asked him.

He hadn't answered her. A fervor of scribbles continued across the pages.

"Jonatan?" she reached across the table and tapped his elbow. He jumped and snapped the notebook closed.

"What?" He exclaimed, running a hand back through his hair.

"What are you writing about?"

"Nothing of relevance to the moment."

The response didn't appease her. "Are you writing about me?"

He opened and closed his mouth a few times, then narrowed his eyes at her. "Why would you think you are at all that interesting to write about?"

Bea sat up straight in her chair, stunned by the rude comment—the second disrespectful remark he had made to her that morning. Heat flooded her face, and without a word, she swiftly gathered the breakfast dishes and clattered them into the sink. When she turned to tell Jonatan that his recent comment was quite hurtful, he was gone. She left the kitchen and walked into the library. Sounds of shuffling and metal banging came from behind Jonatan's closed office door. He had vanished back there without a word or an apology.

B EA TUCKED THE QUILT around the mattress on the floor in Jonatan's second-floor loft, attempting to distract herself from Jonatan's morning attitude. Normally, he was quiet and sullen in the mornings, but today was different. Bea didn't know why, but he was, well, he was mean!

He'd been gone for the past few days. Last night, a loud bang woke her up, followed by a familiar cough. Jonatan returned home long after midnight, and it sounded like he was bringing in a lot of luggage by the way he was fumbling about, grunting and groaning. It was odd because she didn't recall him leaving with anything more than a satchel when he walked toward town to catch the train to Denver City. Bea was far too comfortable in bed to say hello or lend a hand. Besides, she slept in her undergarments since she didn't have proper pajamas. She'd have to get dressed to go downstairs, and then she'd most likely come right back upstairs to undress and return to bed. Her eyes grew heavy at the thought of the effort involved, and she decided she'd see him in the morning over breakfast.

But it wasn't a cheerful hello this morning, and Bea wondered if he had actually slept at all last night, considering that he came to breakfast directly from his office. Her shoulders softened as she smoothed the quilt on her bed after finishing making it. She should give him some grace; he had just returned from another trip. She wasn't sure what the trip was about, but it was probably important.

Bea sat back on her heels and looked around her room. This open space above the library and next to the stairs had become her bedroom. Jonatan hung linen sheets to section off a part of the room, providing her with some much-appreciated privacy.

His bedroom was at the top of the stairs, separated from her converted room by a wall and door. Though her loft was meant to be a future (and additional) library, he never found the time to finish the build, as his practice and research consumed him—a fact to which Bea could attest, given the untidiness of his house. It was surprising because Jonatan appeared very well put together, yet he constantly reminded her of how important his work was, claiming that the frivolity of cleaning would only distract him from his focus. It had been three months since Bea started working for Jonatan, and she couldn't have hoped for anything better. She had housing and meals, though she still hadn't been paid. That was a topic that needed to be addressed soon.

Caring for the house was easy, as Jonatan had simple furnishings, a far cry from the luxury she'd grown up with. The kitchen had the bare necessities to survive, and the parlor only housed Jonatan's extensive book collection, along with a lone rocking chair and side table.

"The *library*," he corrected Bea when she first called it a parlor.

Everything here was calm and simple, and Bea welcomed that feeling. Jonatan mostly treated her with respect, and when he was available for a meal in the kitchen, rather than in his office or away on a trip, he'd invite her to sit with him. They'd spend hours discussing literature, and Bea appeased him by letting him ramble on about his medical practice, even though she didn't follow most of it at first. The human body was quite complex, and she marveled at the cures and remedies offered by the modern medical community, despite the limited advancements available to Jonatan in the remoteness of Yellow Creek City. He relied on his own tools and knowledge; there was no hospital or commune of doctors here to support his endeavors. In any event, she tolerated his ramblings by sitting in silence and taking it all in, knowing she'd understand in time.

But that thought nagged at her. *In time.* How long did she expect to stay here? She had originally planned to leave when she felt she had saved enough money to ensure her stability once she arrived in San Francisco. But since she had yet to be paid, she didn't know how long that would take. Nor did she know exactly how much she would be paid. This was a new venture for her, and she felt that, as a woman, she should be grateful for Jonatan's hospitality so far.

Jonatan was providing her with a free place to sleep and food to eat. And he never asked her for anything more than just being his housekeeper and cook. She no longer had to compromise her morals to survive. Going back to that lifestyle for survival was not one she was eager to return to. But at least that lifestyle paid her in a timely manner, so to speak. Maybe she should start to pressure him....

"Don't look a gift horse in the mouth," she whispered as her thoughts contradicted her. Another word of wisdom from her mother surfaced whenever Bea felt conflicted or scared—words that Bea clung to for guidance and support. It would be best not to apply any pressure just yet, lest Jonatan become annoyed and decide that their arrangement no longer suited him.

She'd give him another month, as she would then be at four months of back pay, which should be more than enough for her needs toward completing her travel and achieving stability. Besides, being in Jonatan's employment wasn't a bad situation at all. She only had two complaints:

one was that she didn't enjoy being left alone when Jonatan traveled.

"Seminars," he'd say, "In Denver City." Those seminars often kept him away for two to three days almost every other week, leaving her alone in this house a mile outside of town. If anything went wrong, there was no one she could reach out to for help. And she especially couldn't go into town, since she wanted to let the townsfolk—more specifically, the sheriff—believe she'd left.

The second complaint is that when Jonatan returned from those trips, he would lock himself away in his office for several days. Bea usually never knew when he had returned as he always arrived in the dead of night. She only knew he was home by the sounds of his coughing and the occasional clanging of metal coming from his office.

Which actually led to a third complaint—she doesn't know what is in that office. It's always locked. Even if she is sitting in the rocking chair in the library and Jonatan leaves that room, he closes the door swiftly behind him, locking it immediately before placing a key in the breast pocket of his vest. He always makes eye contact with her, giving a stern look before nodding his head and departing.

Thinking about what irritated her about Jonatan reignited her anger, reminding her once more of how he had treated her that morning. Bea fluffed her pillow and pounded it flat with her fist. How dare he say something so incredibly rude and then vanish without an apology? He disappeared back to his locked office, where he was doing only the Lord knew what. Bea sighed, weary of the secrecy.

"A doctor's office, my foot," she grumbled. She had yet to see him treat a patient there. Jonatan tended to only make house calls after someone—usually Sheriff Dodson—came to fetch him. And Bea would rarely know the reason for the patient's ailment because, as soon as there was a hint of someone coming down the road toward the house, she'd immediately hide in her room.

Oddly enough, Jonatan requested that she remain unseen by visitors, and Bea didn't know why. However, she didn't question his reasoning because she would prefer it not to be known that she was here. She would rather people believe she left on the train the morning after she arrived.

She sighed and sat back on her heels, the ruffle of her dress shifting underneath her. Bea smoothed the fabric and then touched a hole in the yellow material that had just begun to form above her left knee. Tears welled in her eyes as she thought about how she might wear her mother's yellow dress until it was in rags. She disliked wearing it so much, but it was her only modest dress. The other two were too elegant for her to wear while doing housework.

Why would you think you are at all that interesting to write about? Jonatan's words from the morning echoed in her mind. Tears dripped from her eyes as she clenched her fists in her lap.

"No. I cannot stay here for another month. I just can't." Bea once more countered her own argument. The pay she should have earned to date would have to be enough. She'd make it work—stretching her dollar as far as possible. She didn't deserve to be treated this poorly by anyone—even if they were providing her with room and board. It was time to refocus on her original goal of reaching San Francisco. Bea moved to sit on her bed to ponder how she would approach Jonatan with the request for payment when an anxious female voice yelled from outside the house, ripping her from her thoughts.

"Doc! Doc, can you help us?

Bea crawled over to the window on her hands and knees to peek over the casement. A young blonde girl stood, holding up a much taller and older man. Bea heard the front door open.

"Lily! What's going on?" Bea heard Jonatan ask from beneath the porch roof.

"Pa done cut himself," the girl said. That's when Bea saw that the father had a once-white—now red—strip of linen tied around his hand, which he held clutched to his chest.

"Let me grab my bag, and we'll head back to your place to look at it."

"Doc, please," the man gasped. "I am a bit woozy in my head." He wavered a bit, but the girl held onto him firmly to keep him from falling.

"Doc, he can't walk anymore!" Lily begged.

Bea heard Jonatan curse. Lily pulled her pa forward toward the porch.

"Now, just you wait right there," Jonatan said, his voice sounding unnaturally panicked. The sounds of his footsteps reentered the house.

"Bea!" his voice echoed up the stairs. Bea jumped to her feet and ran to the top of the stairs. Jonatan's face was beet red and glistening. He trembled; a lock of hair fell into his face. With a shaky hand, he pushed it back into place.

"Come down here and sit with Lily and her pa while I set up the office," he disappeared back into the hallway before she could ask any further questions. Bea took a tentative step down, confused by how Jonatan was suddenly okay with her being seen by others. She hesitated on the next step.

To hell with what he wants; I don't want them to know that I'm here, she thought. *What if they see me and start asking questions?* She stopped her descent. A loud groan came from outside.

"Easy, Pa. The doc will be right back," Bea heard the girl say. A wave of pity and guilt washed over Bea. She was focused on her own worries when a man outside was bleeding. Bea took another step. *Don't be silly and selfish. The man is seriously injured, and they aren't going to want to know anything about you.*

Bea took another step, then another. She picked up the pace for the rest of the way down the staircase. As she reached the first floor, she noticed that Jonatan had left the front door open. Lily and her pa remained standing outside. She stepped out onto the porch.

"Hello, why don't you come out of the sun? Come inside and sit," she motioned to them to come forward. Lily smiled and helped her pa slowly up the steps and through the front door. Bea guided them to the rocking chair in the library.

"Jonatan shouldn't be long." The man half-smiled at her. Lily guided her pa to the chair; Bea approached his unattended side and helped him sit. The stink of hot iron radiated off him, and now that she had a closer look, the front of his shirt and chest were soaked in blood from his hand being held against it. Something needed to be done to help him now as the linen wrapping the cut was so saturated that there were a few drops of blood that had followed the man into the house.

Bea recalled Jonatan once saying during one of their dinner conversations that once a cut is wrapped, it should not be unwrapped until it is under a doctor's care. Something about the wrapping being removed from the skin will cause the bleeding to restart or worsen.

"I'll be right back." She went to the kitchen, pulled a dishtowel out of the hutch, and ladled some water from the bucket in the sink into a small tin cup. She took both back into the library. "Here's some water for him. If you can give this to him, I'm going to add some extra wrapping to his hand."

"Thank you, ma'am!" Lily grabbed the cup from Bea and immediately held it to her pa's lips, tipping it back slightly so that he could drink. He drank nearly all of it in one gulp. "We're about two miles from here. It was a long walk."

"Oh my, and there is no shade from the sun out there," Bea said as she gingerly touched the man's exposed and unbloodied forearm, pulling it slightly back from his chest. The man winced. "I'm so sorry. I want to put an extra wrapping around to seep up the blood."

"It's okay, just a little sore," he said, releasing his hand away from his body for Bea. Gingerly, she wrapped the towel around his hand, tightened it, and hoped to slow the bleeding. She had no way to tie it off. "Hold it against your chest again, put some pressure on it; hopefully, that will keep it tight."

"Thank you," the man said.

"What happened?" Bea asked.

"He was showing me how to whet a knife, and it slipped off the rock. Right into his hand," Lily motioned with her hands, sliding the cup across the open palm of her left hand.

Bea's stomach roiled at the thought, but she swallowed hard and smiled. "Jonatan will get you patched right up.

The man cleared his throat. "Aye, he's a good doc."

At that moment, the door to Jonatan's office opened, and he walked out. Sweat poured from his hairline and around his eyes. He wiped at his face and pushed back his hair.

"Okay, Will, come with me," he said, looking at the man.

Will tried to stand, but his legs gave out. Lily and Bea helped him stand. They each held onto an elbow and steered him to Jonatan.

"Is that my dishtowel?" Jonatan asked, nodding at the hand.

"Yes. I'm sorry. He was bleeding through his original bandage. And that's all I could think about to help slow it down."

Jonatan pursed his lips and then gave a satisfied nod. Bea exhaled and looked past Jonatan. The office door stood wide open. Just inside, she could see a silver-colored metal table centered in the room, with a green-globed kerosene lamp hanging above it. Just beyond the table was another closed door. Bea wondered what was behind it.

Will stepped forward. A trill raced up Bea's spine. She was finally going to go inside Jonatan's office!

"I can handle it from here," Jonatan said, reaching out to support Will by his uninjured arm. "Bea, go outside with Lily. We'll be out when I'm done.

"Don't you need help?"

"No," Jonatan said flatly.

"You'll be okay, Pa," Lily said, kissing Will's cheek and then grabbing Bea's hand. "Come on." Bea took one last look through the office door, resisting the tug that pulled her to enter. Oh, how she wanted to see inside that room! But she resisted and followed Lily out of the house.

"Let's go sit in the grass," Lily said softly. "I don't think I could take it if I heard my pa cry. He never cries, but I am sure whatever doc is going to do to him will probably hurt."

Bea's breath hitched before she nodded and led the way out to the small patch of shorter grass to the right of the house. She turned away from Lily so that the girl wouldn't see the tears welling in her eyes. In that moment, Bea missed having a parent—not her father—never her father, but her mother. Watching Lily with her dad intensified the pain of her mother's absence. Bea had never felt more alone in the world than in this moment, realizing what she had missed in not having at least one loving parent in her life. The seven years she had with her mother weren't enough.

The sun shone intensely above, but as it wasn't yet noon, the heat remained bearable. Prairie grass swayed in the breeze, brushing against itself in a soft, swishing melody. Crickets and grasshoppers chirped beneath the stalks, their chorus woven through by the calls of the birds that hunted them. It was peaceful here—quiet in the way only open land could be. Bea lifted her skirt to mid-calf and sat down once they were a little way from the house. Lily followed her lead.

"You family?" Lily asked.

"Pardon?" Bea said, looking at the girl.

"The doc. You his family?"

Bea bit her lip, urging a lie to pass through, "Cousin. Distant cousin." *That would work.*

"Ah, is that why we ain't seen you before?" Lily asked.

"First time to Yellow Creek City. Staying with Jonatan for a couple of months."

"Where you from?"

Bea clasped her hands in her lap, concealing the tremor that racked her fingers. "Oh, um..." she swallowed hard. Lily leaned in toward her, her blue eyes wide with intrigue. The breeze caught the stray wisps of hair that had most likely come loose from her braid during her walk here with Will. Bea chewed the inside of her cheek and watched the wisps glimmer in the sunlight. "Out west," she lied and prayed that would suffice. The girl squinted at her.

"You runnin' from the law?"

"Oh my, no!" Bea was horrified that the girl would even suggest such a thing.

"Ah, you don't have to tell me. I get it." Lily crossed her arms and looked smugly at Bea.

"You...get it?" Bea wasn't quite sure of what Lily was getting at.

Lily winked an eye at Bea. "Man troubles."

Bea burst out laughing, and Lily broke into a huge smile before laughing so hard that she fell backward onto the grass and gazed up at the sky.

"Ever want to fly?" she asked Bea as her laughter subsided.

Bea lay down beside the girl and joined her in watching the clouds, thankful that Lily had changed the subject. "I never really thought about it."

"Me, I want to take my pa and fly far from here. Just me an' him."

"Would you not take anyone else?"

"Naw, my Ma… well, she's fine where she is. With my brothers. Me and Pa are close. I want to take him from here."

"Where would you go?"

"To see the ocean. I heard that you can't see any land beyond the water. You ever see the ocean?"

Bea smiled as she watched the big, puffy clouds float slowly across the crisp blue sky, harkening back to memories of her trips to the Atlantic shore with her mother. "A few times. And what you've heard is true."

"Gosh, did you go in the water?"

"I did," Bea laughed.

"Did you like it?"

"The water was cold. My mother and I would swim until our fingers pruned. But there is something to be said about swimming in vast and endless water, knowing that there is nothing as far as the eye can see. It's like a void to escape into. We'd float in the water and stare at the sky—much like what you and I are doing now."

"That sounds nice," Lily mused.

They lay there for a few moments of silence before Bea asked, "Tell me, if you could fly, how would you fly?"

"Me? I'd grow me some angel wings on my back. Ones with bright and brilliant white feathers so that when me and Pa flew up in the sky, folks would mistake us for clouds."

"You'd carry your pa?"

Lily chuckled. "Shucks no. He'd have big wings, too. Because my daddy is an angel."

Bea swallowed hard and exhaled as tears rolled down her cheeks. She wiped them away so that Lily wouldn't see.

"How would you fly?" Lily asked.

"Pardon?"

"You said you would like to fly, too. How'd you do it?"

Bea chewed her lip as she thought for a moment. The breeze picked up, rippling the grass that sheltered them. She held her hand up to let the breeze wind through her fingers. "I think I would like to let the wind carry me. Carry me to wherever it wanted it to take me."

"You'd have no control over it? Just let the wind decide where you go?"

"Yes, as long as it didn't take me anywhere bad."

Lily shifted, the grass beneath her crackling. "Did your ma come here with you?"

"No." Bea's voice cracked with the answer.

Lily didn't ask any further questions.

They lay in the grass for what felt like hours, watching the clouds drift by and listening to the song of the prairie. Bea's eyes grew heavy from the comfort that surrounded her. Lily had that kind of energy about her—one that calmed Bea, almost making her feel safe. She wished they could be friends, but it wouldn't be wise to make friends in this town. She was only passing through.

"Thanks for sitting with me. I'm worried about my pa, but you helped take my mind off things," Lily said.

"It's been my pleasure. I'm happy I got to meet you, Lily."

"Likewise," Lily said. "Maybe when Pa's hand is better, you and the doc can come to our place for dinner. As a thank you. I'll talk about it with my pa."

"Oh, there is no need for that," the mask of calm slipped from Bea's face. Despite her yearning to befriend this girl, she didn't want to get close. "Jonatan is just doing his job."

"Nonsense, I'll talk to Pa."

Bea sat up and tried to quell the rising panic. "Lily, please—"

"Bea! Lily!" Jonatan's voice shouted from the house. Lily quickly climbed to her feet, and Bea reached out to grab the hem of her dress. The girl dashed toward the house, and the fabric of her dress slipped through Bea's fingertips. Bea exhaled, anxious that the girl would persuade her father to invite them over for dinner. Shielding her eyes, Bea looked toward the house. Jonatan stood on the porch beside Will, who appeared to be smiling with a freshly bandaged hand.

Lily stopped and turned, beckoning Bea with a wave. "Come on now!"

Bea climbed to her feet and walked toward the girl. Lily grabbed Bea's hand. Suddenly, Bea couldn't find the words to tell the girl to forget about dinner. She allowed Lily to pull her into a run, their skirts billowing behind them as the grass crunched beneath their feet. The warm wind whipped Bea's hair back, loosening it from the bun she had pinned that morning. She laughed gleefully alongside Lily, letting her fears catch and float away on the wind.

When they arrived at the porch, that unsettled feeling returned. Both women breathed heavily to catch their breath. Will smiled and hugged his daughter. Jonatan stood unsmiling on the porch; an odd trick of light glinted in his eyes.

"Pa! You're okay!" Lily beamed.

"Just a bit of sewing here from the doc," Will patted the doctor on the shoulder with his unbandaged hand. Bea could still see traces of pain etching Will's sun-worn skin. Jonatan stood like a rock, staring at her.

"Bea. Your hair," Jonatan nodded at the tangled brown strands that hung loosely down to her mid-back.

"I'm sorry," Bea said, hastily gathering it into one hand. She had nothing to pin it back up with, as the pins she had fallen out during the run.

"Oh, pshaw. Don't do that," Lily stepped away from her father and swatted at Bea's hands tangled in her hair. "Let it flow freely!"

She then turned to Jonatan, "Your cousin is a good woman. Let her be."

Anger flickered across Jonatan's face. Bea shifted uncomfortably on her feet as Jonatan continued staring at her, though she was thankful he didn't say anything.

"I'm going in to freshen up. Lily," Bea said, turning to the girl, "It was lovely meeting you. And sir, I hope you heal up quickly." Before Lily or Will could reply, she rushed into the house, and the tears she'd wiped away while she and Lily lay out in the prairie cascaded from her eyes once more.

Chapter 5

IMPERFECT AND IMPROPER

BEA SAT ATOP HER mattress, leaned against the wall, and wept as her fingers worked through the tangled knots in her hair. Once untangled, she used her brush to smooth her hair, restoring its natural shine. Her mother used to sit Bea in front of the vanity mirror and brush her hair repeatedly until the light caught on it like crystal. Bea closed her eyes and imagined that each brush stroke was by her mother's hand.

She sniffed and wiped at her nose and face, clearing it of the sadness. The front door slammed, and Jonatan's heavy footsteps clumped up the stairs. Once at the top, he threw the curtain open and stared at Bea.

"You must always keep your hair up. It's not proper to leave it down," he said to her, the glare still etched on his face. "You look like an imperfect woman."

Bea's fingers tightened around the brush, and for a moment, she worried he might come at her. She swallowed hard; a rare spark of anger ignited in her chest. *An imperfect woman. What does that even mean?*

"I've lost my pins. And also, it isn't improper for a woman to wear their hair down."

"In my house, I expect you to wear it up. I can't have you here looking like that." He flicked his hand at her.

Bea slammed the brush down on the mattress and stood, returning Jonatan's glare, "Then I'll leave once you pay me, and you won't have to deal with *this* any longer."

The angry look on Jonatan's face contorted to shock. "How dare—"

"How dare I?" Bea stood, tossing her hair behind her back as she stepped forward. This situation with Jonatan was no longer tenable, and she was tired of the attitude he directed at her. It reminded her so much of her father. The anger inside her raged into an inferno—anger at how men had controlled every aspect of her life to the point that she could no longer tolerate it. Anger at the fact that she couldn't make a single friend out of fear that her father would find her. Anger at how Jonatan seemed to believe he could dictate what she could and couldn't do with her body.

No. She was going to stand up for herself. "You invited me into your home to help you, promising me pay. I did not come here to be told how I should look or how I should act. I am my own independent woman. I dress however I want. I can act however I want. You have no right to tell me what to do. So, I will say it again—Pay me, and I'll be on my way first thing tomorrow."

Jonatan's face flushed red, and his eyes turned dark. He stepped forward, sucked in a breath, and raised his hand. A cough erupted from his mouth, splattering Bea in the face with spittle. She stood firm and unflinching, continuing to glare at him. She wouldn't give him the satisfaction of reaching out to help. Jonatan doubled over and kept coughing.

Once done, he stood and adjusted his vest by pulling down at the bottom hem. He let go of the fabric and raised his hands to his face. Bea could see red on his fingertips. Jonatan unbuttoned the vest and threw it on the floor at her feet.

"Clean that. It has Will's blood on it." He then turned and stormed to his bedroom, slamming the door behind him.

Bea picked up the corner of the quilt on her bed and wiped Jonatan's cough from her face. When she pulled away the quilt, there was a smear of blood. Bea grabbed her carpet bag and took out her compact mirror. Holding it to her face, she saw no mark that indicated the blood was hers. It was also impossible for her to have gotten Will's blood on her face. She looked toward Jonatan's door and wondered if the blood came from his cough.

Despite her anger toward him, she took a step toward his door, wondering if she should tell him. But she paused. Jonatan was a doctor. Surely, he already knew he was coughing up blood. He would probably be upset with her for mentioning it. And he likely wasn't concerned about it since he was treating Will and was in the company of her and Lily. If he were worried about being contagious or having consumption, as a doctor, he would have quarantined himself. Or at least, Bea hoped he would. Jonatan seemed to be an upstanding doctor who took pride in his work. Being around patients and others while contagious would reflect poorly on him.

Bea decided not to say anything and picked up his vest. She carried it downstairs to the kitchen, grabbed a tin of soap flakes from the hutch, took the pail and washboard from underneath the sink, and then went outside to the water pump to wash Jonatan's vest.

The heat of anger from their argument waned as the rays of sunlight washed over her. That was not the way she wanted to ask about pay, but her question now lingered in the air. She hoped he would reflect on it and act, as she didn't want to bring it up again. Requesting her pay felt unnatural to her.

The handle of the pump was warm and solid in Bea's shaky hands. She needed something to distract her, as she'd been on edge since Jonatan had called her and Lily in after tending to Will's hand.

"Probably my nerves," she mused and then sighed. "It is time for me to go. Tomorrow. I'm sure he will pay me tonight so that I can be gone in the morning."

Bea filled the pail with water and soap, then dunked the vest into the cool ground water, swirling it around. She smiled, content with her decision. The way Jonatan treated her today was a sign that she'd overstayed her welcome. It's like her mother always said, "Guests, like fish, begin to smell after three days." And Bea had been here long past three days.

Once the vest was saturated, she pulled it out and started rubbing it up and down against the washboard. As she pushed the vest down against the board, it rattled as if a stone had gotten caught beneath the fabric. Bea squeezed the vest, trying to find what was causing that noise.

In the breast pocket, Bea's breath caught as she pulled out a key, allowing the sunlight to catch its brassy gold gleam. This key unlocked Jonatan's office. She tucked it into the pocket of her dress's hip fold and resumed washing his vest. Once done, she dumped the water and set the pail and washboard next to the water pump to air dry. She had left the clothesline up from yesterday's wash. Jonatan usually made her take it down after each use because it was attached to the side of the house to a pole in the yard, but she honestly forgot to put it away. Bea draped the vest over the cloth line to let it dry in the afternoon sun. Then she returned to the house.

Bea quietly entered the house and removed her shoes. She then padded softly up the stairs to Jonatan's room and placed her ear against the door. From the other side, she heard snores. A smile spread across her face, confirming that he had lain down for an afternoon nap. Bea quietly crept back downstairs, turned left into the library, and then took another left into the hallway beside the stairs.

She pressed her left hand's fingertips against the office door and grasped the doorknob with her right hand. After twisting it, she confirmed that it was locked. The key slid smoothly into the keyhole, and the lock clicked open with a turn of the key. The doorknob turned effortlessly.

Bea creaked the door open. Jonatan had left the kerosene lamp burning above the long metal table in the room. To the left of the metal table was a wooden countertop with drawers beneath and cabinets hanging above. Several books and a collection of sharp-looking objects were stacked on the counter. Next to the metal table stood a smaller one that held other instruments and bloodied gauze. Bea imagined Lily's Pa lying on the long metal table while Jonatan stitched up his hand.

A small wooden table and two chairs were positioned on the right side of the room, directly in front of Bea, who stood in the open doorway.

"Ah, so this is where you eat when you bring your meals in here," Bea whispered as she stepped into the room and ran her hand along the back of the nearest wooden chair. A closed door was situated on the far side of the room, directly opposite where she stood.

Overall, Jonatan's office was sparse, and Bea appreciated that he kept things neat and orderly. She didn't want to rummage through his cabinet and drawers but assumed that was where he stored his instruments.

But the door at the other side of the room—something there beckoned to her curiosity. She wanted to know what he kept inside. Bea swiftly walked across the floorboards to the door at the back of the room. Without thinking, she grabbed the doorknob and twisted—unlocked. A smile crept across her face as she wondered what kind of interesting secrets the doctor had hidden inside.

Bea slowly opened the door. The room was dark. As she opened the door partially, light from a single kerosene lamp spilled in, creating a beam on the floor. Two bare legs with feet pointing to the ceiling lay starkly in the light. Bea jumped at the sight and swung the door wide open, fully illuminating the room.

The scream that erupted from her throat couldn't be controlled. She screamed and screamed and screamed as she stared at the form of a woman sitting upright in the small room. Her blonde head tilted to the side, hair cascading down over her naked body. Her eyes were dull, grey, and lifeless.

Bea was yanked backwards by her hair. Twisting, Jonatan stood behind her, his eyes blazing. He raised his free hand, clutching a syringe between his fingers. A sharp, stinging sensation jabbed at Bea's neck, sending warmth flooding through her body. Her eyes grew heavy, and then it registered that Jonatan had stabbed her in the neck with the syringe, emptying the contents into her body. She felt like a sack of coal, and her legs lost their strength. Before collapsing, she vomited down the front of her yellow dress and onto the floor.

Chapter 6

SOILED DOVES

B EA WOKE UP PARALYZED. While she could move her eyes and breathe, she couldn't move any part of her body. All she could do was stare at the green-globe, brass kerosene lamp hanging above her and feel coldness beneath her. She tried to remain calm, but panic flared. Her breathing quickened. She looked around, trying to see anything beyond the lamp and wooden ceiling. From what she could tell, the walls and the ceiling were made of the same material, raw and unpainted. She could barely make out a table and cabinets in the periphery on her right.

"This won't do." A man's voice spoke above her head. A face appeared over her, and she felt him softly touch her neck, followed by a sharp stab. He looked familiar. "I'm sorry."

The cold evaporatcd. Bca flushed with warmth and drifted off to sleep.

B EA FELT HER ARM rise and her fingers touch her temple. *She could move.* Bea sat up and shivered at the thought of the dream in which she'd felt paralyzed. And that man. She couldn't quite remember who he was, although he seemed familiar. She exhaled, trying to ease the headache that throbbed on the side of her head. Once that subsided, she untangled her legs from the sheet covering her.

The bed beneath her felt off.

Bea tried to stand, but as she threw her legs over what she thought was the edge of the mattress, she discovered her feet were on the floor. Beneath her lay a tangled pile of sheets. Light filtered through a crack under the door and from a hole to the right of the doorknob. As her eyes adjusted, she found herself in an empty room that was slightly longer than her height in both directions. She noticed she was dressed in a pair of tattered linen pants and a button-down shirt—clothes that weren't hers. *Where was her dress?*

Bea pulled herself up to the wall nearest to her. A wave of nausea washed over her, sweeping away any further thoughts about what had happened to her clothes. She swallowed hard to keep from throwing up. Her wobbly legs reminded her of the paralysis dream. Using the wall for support, she shuffled to the door while hiking up the pants that had drifted off her hips.

From there, she peeked through the small hole. The room outside was larger, with a table standing in the center beneath a familiar glass-globe lamp. In the haze of her memory, she realized she had seen this room once before. Something lay on the table, draped with a white sheet.

She fumbled with the doorknob. Locked. "The man," Bea whispered as she remembered the face peering over her in her "dream". *Jonatan.* A cold shiver shook her body. *What did he do to me?*

"Help!" Bea screamed as she pounded the palms of her hands against the door. "Please! Someone help me!"

When the screaming brought no one, she slammed her body against the door, trying to burst it open. But her stature was too light to even make the door shudder in its frame. Turning her back to the door, she slid down it until she sat on the floor. She pulled her knees to her chest and wept into them. "Please..."

No. She chided herself. *Do not just sit here, waiting for someone to come.*

She stood back up and tried to open the door again. If the hinges had been on her side, she might've been able to pry the pin out of the hinge and break out that way. In the little light she had, Bea knelt and ran her hands along the baseboards. She pressed her fingernails into the crack between the baseboard and the wall to see if she could pry any up. When that produced no results, she ran her hands all over the empty walls, reaching as high as she could. She was unable to touch the ceiling.

Her hand bumped into something that shifted, and light briefly filtered in before disappearing behind what she had moved. Squinting, she could make out a square of wood, no thicker than an inch, nailed to the top of the wall. She pushed the piece of wood, and it slid sideways, revealing a hole to the outside. It was big enough for both of her eyes to look through. A summer breeze swept in, causing her to flinch and close her eyes as she breathed in the fresh air.

Bea opened her eyes and looked out across the muted green and brown prairie, with blades of grass dancing under the hazy purplish-blue sky. The sun wasn't visible, but it was rising somewhere to her left or behind her, which meant that she must be facing north or east. Not that it mattered much now; she had a sense of where she might be. She was in the small room at the back of Jonatan's office.

The noise of another door opening outside where she was trapped made her jump. She dropped the wooden slat, which swung back and forth on its nail over the hole. Bea steadied it with her hand and then retreated to the pile of sheets.

Footsteps came from the other side of her door, accompanied by a clatter of glass and the thud of cabinets opening and closing. There was whispering that Bea couldn't decipher. For a moment, she wondered if there were two people in the room. She cautiously moved to the door to peek through the small open knothole in the wood near the doorknob. Jonatan was pacing about the room. His hair was slicked back, and he was dressed in his usual attire—including his vest. Bea found that quite strange because she had just left it to dry outside. It had to be still fairly wet. *Why was he wearing a damp vest?*

A cough from her own chest nearly revealed that she was watching him as she realized she was holding her breath.

The secret is to keep breathing, she mentally repeated, to calm herself and stifle her nerves so she could continue watching without provoking him.

Jonatan walked toward her, carrying a metal tray. Glass rattled. Bea scooted backward to the pile of sheets. She didn't want to be caught looking through the hole. The door opened, and she squinted from the additional light pouring into the small room, which silhouetted him. He stepped inside with a tray holding a glass of water, a bowl of soup, and a spoon.

Bea stood as her vision adjusted to the light. Their eyes met, but neither spoke. She took a cautious step forward.

"What are you doing?" she asked, voice trembling.

He stood in the open doorframe. "I need you to stay in here."

"Jonatan, I don't understand. Let me go. I won't tell any-one. I promise."

"No." He stepped forward.

Bea leaned to the left and looked around his shoulder, seeing an exit to flee to as he'd left the door to the library wide open. Then she looked at the center table, at the sheet draped over whatever lay beneath it. The center of the sheet was splattered with crimson.

She gasped, taken by surprise. "Is that blood?"

He lifted his leg—while balancing the tray—and kicked her in the stomach, sending her backward. Bea's head struck the wall. Stars blurred her vision but faded as quickly as they had appeared. Jonatan placed the tray on the floor and stepped back into the light. The door slammed shut.

"HELP!" Bea screamed. She turned and pounded her hands against the back wall. "HEEELLP!"

"You can stop that right now," Jonatan said from the other side of the door. "You know full well how far we are from town. No one will hear you."

"Please," she sniffed. "Please let me go. I won't tell anyone what happened, promise. I'll leave, and you don't even have to pay me."

Nothing more was said from the other side of the door. She tried to negotiate with him for what felt like hours until her voice grew hoarse. Bea curled up on the pile of sheets and watched the light flicker through the gap at the bottom of the door. She listened to him busying himself out there. From time to time, he would cough or clear his throat.

She needed to reach him somehow—because she didn't understand what he was doing or why she was in this room. "What are you doing out there?"

Silence. A lump in her throat pulsed, willing tears to spring from her eyes. With a shaky hand, she pressed her fingertips to her lips to stifle her crying. She didn't want him to know she was afraid.

"I'm performing an autopsy," he replied.

Bea jolted upright at the sound of his voice. He had responded to her, and she wasn't about to lose this connection. "A what?"

"An autopsy. That's what the blood is from."

Bea inhaled sharply, remembering the woman she'd seen in the closet at the back of his office. She jumped to her feet, realizing she'd been sitting where she'd seen the body.

"That woman was in here," Bea slammed herself against the door. "Please, Jonatan, let me out of here."

She heard him walk up to the door, ignoring her plea. "The woman, she died. I'm dissecting her body for re-search."

"You cut open bodies?" Bea whispered. She shook. "Is that...is that what you've been doing in here all this time? Is that what you are going to do to me?"

Jonatan walked away from the door. After a few moments, he said in a flat tone, "No. I don't think I'll be doing that to you now."

He won't be doing that to me... now? Bea didn't want to anger him by asking more questions; he might change his mind. Yet the question gnawed at her. *What exactly was he going to do with her?*

That was not a question she wanted to know the answer to. She needed to find a way to escape. As she forced herself not to think about his motives, her stomach growled. She looked at the soup, hesitant to trust it, wondering if he'd slipped something into it. Still, the hunger roaring in her belly made it feel like days had passed since she last ate.

Hearing the door in the other room open and close, Bea hurried to her door to peek through the hole. Jonatan had left the room, but atop the table still lay the body, covered with a white sheet. The kerosene lamp cast its light around the windowless room, giving Bea a clear view of everything.

"Ohhhhh," she sighed and closed her eyes. "Just breathe, just breathe." Anxiety washed over her as she thought about a dead body in the other room. She was sharing space with a dead body.

"The secret is to keep breathing," a calm, level voice said.

Those words were her mother's, but it wasn't her voice, nor did the statement come from Bea. She jumped and looked around her prison before looking back through the hole. No living being was present in the area, as she could see. Yet, someone had uttered those words.

"Hello?" Bea called out.

The other room stood still and silent. Bea sat back on her heels and placed a hand on her forehead, worried that she was starting to hear things.

"The secret is to keep breathing."

"Hello?" Bea scrambled back to her little window into the next room. "Please, is there someone there? Help me."

Again, she was met with silence as she scanned the room. A slight ripple in the section of the sheet that draped over the woman's head caused Bea to yelp. She covered her mouth with her hands and fell backward. "You're hearing things," Bea told herself, then rolled onto her side, clutching her chest. "She's dead. The dead don't talk."

She repeated this mantra until her heart rate returned to a normal beat and she began to feel grounded. "You're hungry. You're delusional. You're scared." Bea tried to coax herself to a calmer place. "Let's eat and think of a plan on how to get out of here, okay?"

The sound of just her own voice speaking and no one else was relieving. She rationalized her situation. There was no one in the other room who could help. She need-ed to think through how to get out. These two rooms had no windows and, she assumed, two locked doors she needed to get through.

Jonatan said he wasn't going to kill her, and hopefully that also meant he wouldn't hurt her either.

"Oh my," she cried, leaning her forehead against the door. How could she have trusted him so? Blindly trusted him. Bea really didn't know him at all. And that woman. What about that woman? Did he...? No! She couldn't let herself think about it.

Bea needed to remain level-headed and calm around him. It was the same as with her father; he would leave her alone when she didn't fight or push back.

"Just do what he says and watch for a way out." Bea exhaled. She repeated the statement three more times to convince herself that it was the right thing to do.

Hunger burbled in her stomach again. She shifted her focus to distract her mind from dwelling on what lay on the other side of her door. Bea picked up the tray and carried it to her makeshift bed. Placing it on the floorboards before her pile of sheets, she grabbed the glass of water and gulped it down—only realizing how thirsty she was after the last drop rehydrated her parched throat. She stirred the spoon through the white, black-speckled soup.

It had congealed and cooled since he'd set the tray down. She was relieved that the room wasn't bright enough to reveal the exact type of soup, and she hoped the speckles she could see were just pepper. She picked up the spoon and slowly sipped it. Cold and unappetizing—it at least staved off her hunger pains.

Thunder rumbled outside the wall as a storm approached. Bea settled back into the sheets once she could no longer tolerate the congealed texture of the soup and listened to the rain pelting the roof. A wave of nervousness washed over her.

"Don't have bad thoughts. He's not going to hurt you," Bea told herself through quick and panicked breaths. "Jonatan said that isn't what he was going to do with you now."

But did it mean that, at one point, he had considered it? And what would he do to her now?

B EA DIDN'T KNOW THE time. She didn't know if it was night or day or how long she'd been lying—wide awake and in terror—on the sheet pile as she hid in her safe place. A place where no one could hurt her. It was silent on the other side of the door.

She needed to find a way to escape. There had to be an option other than getting through two doors—which she assumed were both locked. Another solution had to exist. She slid over to the door. Pressing her ear against the wood, silence urged her bravery. She peered through the small hole next to the knob. The room remained mostly empty until Bea's sight settled in the middle of the room... and she screamed.

The sheet that covered the woman's body lay in a pile on the floor to the right table—tangled blonde locks hung from the table, flanked by pale shoulders.

The room temperature seemingly dropped as the realization washed over Bea that Jonatan had not returned to the room, yet this woman now lay fully exposed on the table. Bea dropped her gaze to the floor beneath the table to try to rationalize what had happened to the sheet. That was when she noticed a red puddle no bigger than a dinner plate. She turned, grabbed the empty soup bowl from the tray behind her, and hurled up her dinner. Her vomit hit the bowl and sloshed out, covering the sheets, the floor, her feet, and clothes.

With an acidic taste in her mouth, she began to breathe sharply and quickly. The stench of her vomit, combined with the overwhelming sight of it, made her feel woozy. The light from the crack in the door started to swirl. A long, guttural scream she could not control tore past her lips. Her vision flared a bright gold. Moments later, something cold and damp was wiping her face, neck, and hands.

"I'm sorry." It was Jonatan.

Bea's eyes rolled, and everything came into focus as she forced herself not to faint. Jonatan looked at her with pity as he wiped her clean. Bea shuddered at his touch, pushing him away. She rotated to her right and climbed to her feet. He took a step back, leaving an opening in the doorway. Bea saw her chance and bolted forward, but her foot slipped in her vomit. She crashed against the door jamb. Righting herself, she took three slippery steps out of the room and stopped before the body.

The woman was young. Her face was a pale, blueish grey. A dark gash marred her throat. Deep and hollow, red flesh exposed. And her chest and stomach... the entire cavity had been opened, exposing the woman's insides.

Run! Bea's mind screamed. Before the words could register, arms surrounded her. She threw her head backward, connecting with Jonatan's face. He dropped her. As she stepped forward, her foot slipped on the vomit that she'd trailed out from the closet. She fell, striking her forehead on the edge of the autopsy table.

Chapter 7

Hypothesis

THE SOUND OF SOMETHING soft being cut annoyed Bea. Her head felt heavy as she allowed it to lull to one side and then the other, trying to turn away from the sound. She wanted to sleep, but the noise was irritating. Bea raised her hand to rub her eyes, and upon realizing she couldn't move her arms, she immediately woke up to find herself tied to a chair—in the other room this time. Jonatan stooped over the brown-haired woman.

Brown hair?

"Where did the blonde woman go?" she asked.

"Who?" He cleared his throat, a rough cough cutting the silence. The sound of metal meeting metal echoed as he set something down on the table next to the woman. He stuck his fingertips into her chest, never once looking away from the body.

The bile rose in the back of Bea's throat as he forced his hands into her chest. The sharp crack of ribs hung heavy in the air. A shiver raced up and down her spine as she flexed her bound wrists, trying to slip the bonds that held her to the chair.

A heaviness settled in her stomach at the sticky, wet sound of organs being roughly handled. Her head dropped forward before snapping back up to attention. *Breathe, breathe, breathe,* she instructed herself. She needed to get out of here.

Jonatan removed his bloodied hands and turned to a small table on his left that held a notebook, a pencil, and an array of sharp-looking tools. Bea could see red stains on the paper and the pencil itself. He didn't wipe his hands before using these tools; yet, he cursed as a bloody smear streaked across the page.

Bea closed her eyes and swallowed hard, trying to ignore the sight and smell of blood. "The blonde-haired woman. This one's different."

"I was done with her."

"What did you do with her?"

"I buried her."

"What happened to this one?"

"She died too. This is another autopsy."

Sitting behind the woman's head, Bea couldn't see her neck. But she wanted to. She wanted to see if she had the same cut across the throat. *Did these women die the same way?*

"Can I see?"

"No." He closed his notebook, the cover also stained with blood. Turning to the washbasin on the counter behind him, Jonatan washed his hands and then draped the woman's body with a white sheet before walking over to Bea.

She looked down at her clothes—a blue button-down shirt and gray slacks. "You changed me?"

"You were covered in vomit," he said.

Her shirt and slacks felt oddly different, yet comfortable. These clothes were not as confining as a dress. *Her mother's dress!* Bea remembered wearing it the day she unlocked Jonatan's office.

"Where is my yellow dress? Why am I in your clothes?" she demanded.

"I threw out your dress and had nothing else to put you in." He stepped beside her, picking up a bowl and spoon. She hadn't noticed the soup bowl to her left before. "You won't throw this up again, will you?"

"My dress... is gone?" Bea's voice cracked, and her face flushed hot. "That was my mother's dress." She couldn't hold back the tears, crying a mournful sob at the loss of one of her mother's belongings.

"Bea," Jonatan said sternly, "Get ahold of yourself. It was only an article of clothing."

This made Bea cry harder. So much had been taken from her over and over again, all by the hands of men.

"BEA!" Jonatan shouted. She glared up at him, hate pulsating behind her eyes. Pulling the bowl back toward his chest, Jonatan recoiled. For a moment, she believed he feared her.

"There will be no more of this blubbering. You will eat or you will starve." He stepped forward, coming back into her space. Bea wanted to snatch the bowl from his hands and smash it over his head.

"The secret is to keep breathing." The words whispered in the air and hung heavily between them. They had not come from her mouth. Bea averted her gaze from Jonatan and

looked behind him at the sheet. She swore she saw it ripple across the face hidden beneath it.

Bea inhaled and exhaled. She could bide her time. There was nothing she could do in this moment but comply and eat. But once she has a chance to escape, she'll take it by any means necessary.

As if she sensed her compliance, Jonatan dipped the spoon into the soup, ladled a translucent brown broth, and then brought it to her lips. At first, she resisted his gesture—small lines of blood still streaked his hands—but then her stomach growled, reminding her of how she'd vomited her previous meal. She sipped from the spoon. Though bland, it filled her.

"There we are." He smiled. "I'm sorry for all of this."

A tear slid down Bea's cheek. "Why are you doing this to me?"

"I needed a control in my research."

"Your research?"

"I'm conducting research on the female anatomy to identify the physical traits that lead some women into lives of sin. This one, and the one before her, were prostitutes who passed."

"But you invited me into your home—to work for you! Why not just rob a grave of a well-bred woman?"

"There are not many women like you in these parts." He smiled. "I knew that the moment I met you at The Claim. So I watched. Observed you over the months, just to be sure. You are the perfect, untainted specimen."

Bea glared at him, remembering her suspicions as he scribbled in his notebook in her presence. "You were taking notes about me all this time! And lied to me when I questioned you about it. How long were you going to string me along?"

He remained silent as he ladled another spoonful of broth. Bea turned her head away, refusing to eat any more unless he answered her questions.

"Bea, I need you to eat."

"I asked you a question," she spat. "How long were you going to watch me?"

"I don't know how long I was going to study you before bringing you in here," Jonatan said, putting the spoon down and running his hands through his hair, frazzled. "After you yelled at me upstairs, I considered paying you that night and letting you go. Because... well, that doesn't matter anymore since you saw what I'm doing here, and I can't have this information shared yet. My research hasn't been completed. And now I want your help to finish it."

"You first wanted to kill and cut me up. Then you were going to let me go." She nodded toward the dead woman's body. "Now you've locked me up and want my help?"

He sighed. "I've been reflecting on you a lot over these past several days since you've been in here."

"Days? I've been in here for days?" Anger flushed her face, burning her cheeks.

"Bea, I haven't met anyone as intellectual as you in this town," he said. "And I can't keep doing this work on my own. It's too much for one person to handle. I've been pondering heavily on this while spending the past few days alone."

"What?" Bea said, not following what he was saying.

He knelt in front of her and took one of her bound hands in his own. "My research is suffering due to a lack of evidence for my hypothesis. I needed a control specimen for comparison. That was to be you."

He let go of her hand and stood, towering over her.

Memories of how she met Jonatan swirled in her mind. She hadn't thought about this before, but everything seemed to line up perfectly—too perfectly. It was as if he had seen her arrive in town and had planned this the moment he spotted her. Yet, that felt like a bit too much of a stretch to believe.

Sheriff Dodson. A tremor wracked Bea's body as she thought about that vile man. *What if he set this up? Does he know what Jonatan is doing? What if he ran to Jonatan's place right after I left and told Jonatan to abduct me—to kill me and get his money back?*

The room grew hot and stuffy, suffocating. A bead of sweat dripped from Bea's hairline next to her right ear and ran down to her jaw.

"But as I said, you're too intelligent to be used as a specimen," Jonatan rambled on. "I've decided to use you to help me with my research. You'll stay here and take my notes for me." He raised a hand toward his notebook. "As you can see, it's too messy for me to perform the autopsy and write down my findings."

The room shifted as Bea tried to grasp what he was saying. "And what is your research again?"

He glared at her, seemingly annoyed at having to repeat himself. "My research is to find why women choose to embark on a life of sin by selling their bodies. I hypothesize there is something tangible inside of a woman that makes her walk down the road toward Satan. It's physical, not metaphysical. It's a cancer, a clump of cells inserted into each body by the devil as his mark and found only in women who worship him as their savior. Good Christian women of society lack these cells."

Bea bit her lip, holding back from admitting she was one of those women. If she did, she'd be next on the table. Maybe Sheriff Dodson hadn't told Jonatan about her after all. Surely, he would have revealed to Jonatan that she'd provided him services the evening she came to work for Jonatan. She would've long been killed, dissected, and buried. Maybe it was the other man at the train station that day? She bent her head to the right and closed her eyes, trying to remember the man's name. *Jessup.* It had to be the man sleeping on the train station platform.

Honestly, it didn't matter how she ended up in this situation. What mattered was that she needed to get out of it.

"In addition to you taking my notes," he paused and seemed to consider his next words, "I would like to continue the conversations that we often had. I find myself looking forward to those times. There's no one else in this town I can talk to on an academic level."

Bea seethed. Their conversations were mostly one-sided, with Jonatan doing all the talking; whenever she spoke up, she was told she was wrong. However, Bea sat in rapt attention because she was interested in what he had to say. Jonatan was quite knowledgeable. During evening mealtimes, he wasn't eating in this room to "work." Instead, they would sit together in the kitchen and chat into the late hours of the evening about literature, science, and anatomy.

"If, in the end, you just wanted a smart conversation and a little help documenting your notes, you should be upfront about what you are doing."

Jonatan stepped back and looked at the floor, staring so intently that Bea thought he'd burn a hole in the ground. "Bea, you must understand how hard this is for me. I only saw you initially as a test subject. But I feel as though we have bonded in a way I've never bonded with anyone in my life. I need your friendship. And I was...I was afraid."

Bea shot forward in the seat as far as the restraints would allow, "Afraid I'd hightail it out of here the moment I learned you were going to dissect me? Afraid I'd run right to the sheriff?"

The latter statement elicited a small smile on Jonatan's lips before they flatlined again. "To be honest, while I do need a control subject, and while that was my original intent, I changed my mind over the time you've been in this room."

"Your story keeps changing ever so slightly, Jonatan. When will you be honest with me? You seem to want my companionship. Well, I need honesty."

"Friendship. I want your friendship. I'm in no need of companionship. That has never interested me."

"Then, if you want my friendship, be honest. What are you going to do with me?"

"I've already told you; I want you to stay here as my assistant."

"You can't keep me tied to this chair forever."

"On that, we agree. I won't. You need to have your hands free to assist me."

"Fine. The next question you need to answer honestly: how do you obtain these women?"

Jonatan grabbed the back of the chair and moved her away from the door, ignoring her question.

"No, no, no. Please don't put me back in there," Bea cried.

He opened the door. From what she could see, the room was free of her vomit and dirty sheets. Her mattress from upstairs—quilt and all—now rested on the floor, and he'd added a small table with a kerosene lamp on top.

"Please, no," her voice cracked. You said you needed my help. Don't lock me back up in there!"

"You misunderstand." Jonatan coughed, then pulled a long, thick metal chain from the closet. He brought it to her, fastening a heavy metal shackle around her ankle, and removed the key from the lock. He then produced a second key from his breast pocket.

Bea bit her lip. That had to be the office key, since it was in the same pocket where she'd found a key while laundering his vest. There was a piece of twine now tied to the office key, which he linked to the shackle key—joining both together. He then returned both keys to his breast pocket before leaning down to untie her feet and hands. Once her wrists and ankles were unbound, she stood and went into the closet to find the end of the chain bolted to the back wall.

In addition to the table, lamp, and mattress, Jonatan added a chamber pot on the floor along with extra blankets inside the room. He had not touched the hole above the lamp. It still had the flat piece of wood nailed to it—her only window to the outside. Bea pulled at the chain against the wall.

"I'm allowing you free rein in my office and this closet that is now your new bedroom," Jonatan had returned to his notebook on the small table beside where the woman lay. Bea tugged at the chain.

"You're locking me in these rooms?" she tugged harder. "You can't imprison me here!"

"*Don't waste your energy.*"

Bea dropped the chain and jumped to her feet as she heard a woman's voice—different from the one before. Spinning around, she saw Jonatan with a knife in one hand while pulling the sheet off the woman with the other.

"What did you say?" She looked at the woman.

"What?" Jonatan looked up at Bea.

"I thought I heard someone say something. A woman." She looked down at the body he'd returned to, then at him.

He cocked an eyebrow.

"*No escape.*"

"There!" Bea jumped.

Jonatan cleared his throat and set down his knife. "I think you need rest." He covered the body with the sheet, but left her head exposed.

"Don't leave me here with...!" Bea breathed hard and nodded toward the body. She backed into the small room as her body lit with fear. Then, she glanced at the kerosene lamp. If she could light it, she'd have fire...

Jonatan stood by the door.

"I know what you're thinking, and you can stop that. Don't try to burn the place. You won't be able to escape. These walls are thick."

He tapped the wall closest to him with his finger.

"And that door is the only way out." He nodded to the door that led out of his office.

"I wasn't thinking that," she lied, trying to act composed. Yet, thoughts of how she might escape through the office door lingered in her mind. To demonstrate that escape wasn't on her mind, she walked out of the closet, dragging the chain behind her, and stood at the woman's head.

The woman had bruising on her face just under her right eye. The same gash opened her throat. Bea began to suspect these women weren't dying of natural causes.

"Did you kill her?" she whispered. Bea raised a hand to pat the bruise but resisted touching the skin as familiarity with abuse crawled all over her skin.

Jonatan walked over and grabbed her arm. His icy hands were thin yet strong. She could feel the muscle in his grip. He pushed her back into the closet—the shackle, heavy around her ankle, dragged the chain along. Shoving her and the chain inside, he slammed the door behind her. Bea stared at the closed door.

Jonatan cleared his throat. "I'm retiring for the evening. Good night."

The sound of the office door closing with a metallic *click* jolted Bea from her trance. She grasped the doorknob in front of her; discovering it was unlocked, she flung it open and rushed toward the locked office door.

"Don't leave me alone here with her!" Bea screamed.

"*Safer here. Just keep breathing.*"

Bea whirled around, the chain rattling against the ground with her movement. She stared at the woman's head poking above the sheet.

"How are you talking?" Bea cried.

The corpse made no response.

Bea's breath caught in her chest, and she couldn't inhale. Couldn't exhale. This room was too small, with its heavy, rancid air. She ran back to the tiny room, past the dead woman, and tried to slam the closet door shut, but the chain wasn't all the way through. Bea grasped the part that was outside the entrance and pulled it back as quickly as she could.

Once fully inside, she slammed the door shut. Gooseflesh covered her arms and legs. Ghosts. There was a ghost in the office. Here for her because she had sinned. Bea's shaking became so uncontrollable that she knew she'd fall. Turning, she faced the hole in the wall and moved the piece of wood out of the way.

A half-moon hung high in the dark, star-speckled sky. The breeze danced waves of silver across the prairie grass. Nothingness beckoned her—whispers of escape to the mountains and beyond.

But how could she escape? There were no windows in this room—or the next—except for this hole to the outside, which must have been an access vent for an old chimney pipe. Jonatan wasn't lying. The walls of her prison were thick; she could see the depth through this hole. Access to the outside world was behind two doors. It was as if these rooms had been purposely built.

For what, Bea could only imagine—but tried not to as death invaded her thoughts. How she wished she had paid more attention to how the exterior was laid out around Jonatan's house. Maybe she would have seen another means of escape: a trap door or something. Bea never saw him bring these women into the house, so she found it hard to believe that he was sneaking them in through the front door.

"Oh, my goodness," Bea gasped, holding a hand to her mouth to suppress any other loud noises from escaping, so as not to alert the ghost.

His trips—Jonatan was supposedly going to seminars for all those trips to Denver City. He never went to seminars but was probably collecting bodies from whoever was selling them to him, doing it under the cover of night. Bea had always been a heavy sleeper, sleeping through his return. Her breath shook as she exhaled, and it took effort to inhale.

"The secret is to keep breathing." Bea placed her hand on her chest and repeated the words once spoken by her mother to help shift her focus away from Jonatan and the possibility that the ghosts of these women haunted these walls.

The secret is to keep breathing. The first time Bea heard those words, her mother was sitting at her vanity table, applying a colored cream that matched her skin to the purplish discoloration under her left eye and cheekbone. Earlier that day, her parents had been arguing in the foyer before the grand staircase. Bea watched the entire event from the second-floor landing. She never understood why they were fighting, but the outcome was her father punching her mother in the face. A younger Bea would have screamed and tried to defend her mother. The six-year-old Bea, who watched the attack, slunk backward from the banister, crying, knowing full well that if she intervened, she would suffer the same fate.

"The secret is to keep breathing, sweetie," her mother said as she applied the flesh-cream to hide the bruises. "It's the only way women survive this terrible world."

Bea breathed in deeply before exhaling. A rational mind was necessary. If there were ghosts and it wasn't just her mind playing tricks, they weren't doing anything but talking. And with Jonatan, she needed to play this smart and safe. Jonatan was intelligent, and the only way to overthrow him was to trick him. She knew what she needed to do: she needed to get him to trust her.

Chapter 8

THE FIRST CUT

HEAVY FOOTSTEPS AND MUFFLED voices echoed from beyond the door. Bea rose from her place on the floor and approached the door. It remained unlocked. She cracked it open and peeked into the other room. The light above the metal table showed that the woman was gone. The room was empty. Jonatan must have returned while she slept and taken the woman away. Either he was cautious in his movements, or Bea was so exhausted that she had been fast asleep. In any case, she smiled as she fully opened the door and walked into the room.

The air felt lighter, not as heavy and hot as it had been inside the closet. She glanced at the door on the opposite side of the room, pondering whether it was also unlocked. As she took a step forward, the chain around her ankle rattled. Defeated, she sighed, her head falling forward. At her feet, wet spots formed from the tears dripping from her eyes. Even if the door were unlocked, she'd still be chained in place.

Bea lifted her head and wiped her eyes. She sighed and began moving toward the chair beside her when Jonatan barged in and quickly closed the door behind him. He exhaled and then locked eyes with Bea.

"Get back in that room and keep quiet." He hissed at her. His hair stood in various directions, not slicked back as usual.

"What?" Bea said, stepping backward toward the closet, dragging the chain along the floor.

His eyebrows knitted in anger as he moved forward and forced her into the closet, kicking the chain in after her. Bea stumbled and fell onto the mattress. Jonatan slammed the door shut, and at the sound of metal touching metal, Bea heard the lock click into place.

"Jon—"

"Quiet," he said in a sharp whisper.

"What's going on?"

"Do not speak. Do not make any movement. Keep as still as possible."

"Why?"

He sighed. "I have a patient."

Bea's heart fluttered. Someone else was here. She breathed in, ready to scream for help, when Jonatan hissed through the door, "Scream, and I'll kill them."

Bea clamped her lips tight. Her chin trembled. She had no idea how many people were out there. If there were more than one, they could easily overpower Jonatan. But if only one person was outside, Jonatan could quickly kill them—and it would be Bea's fault. She slid forward on the mattress and pressed her ear against the door, straining to listen for any sounds of multiple people beyond these two rooms. She shifted in her crouch as the cuff around her ankle pinched her skin. The chain rattled.

"I told you not to move," he said. Unsure of what to do, Bea sat back on the mattress and contemplated her options.

Jonatan walked away from the door and began opening cabinets. The sounds of glass vials and metal trays clattering were followed by footsteps returning to the door.

"Make any sound, and I'll kill them," he reminded her.

Bea wasn't sure if he was lying. Although she couldn't tell if it was a veiled threat, she couldn't hear outside the rooms to confirm who was truly there and couldn't risk anyone getting hurt. However, she also couldn't remain a prisoner here. She had come to know Jonatan as steadfast in his decisions. He'd never waver and let her go. But she didn't believe he would actually harm a patient, as that would permanently damage his reputation.

She needed to signal to whoever was in the house without Jonatan noticing. Bea chewed her lip before crawling forward as quietly as possible to avoid rattling the chain around her ankle. Through the small hole in the door, she observed Jonatan gathering his medical supplies before opening the other door. Darkness framed the doorway, but just beyond, a yellowish-orange glow flickered off the walls. Nighttime. That meant the patient had traveled here at night for help.

A fit of coughs drifted through the door.

"Lily, I'm coming right now with some medicine," Jonatan said with a soft and sweet tone. He held a vial of medicine in his left hand. Bea's heart seized. In a lower voice, he said to Bea, "And you are no longer here if she asks. Gone off to who knows where."

Lily.

Lily was Jonatan's patient.

Bea froze. She couldn't bring herself to make any movement or noise to call attention to herself, fearing that her actions might backfire and harm Lily. Despite knowing rationally that the girl would never have come here at night on her own, and realizing that someone must have brought her, Bea was uncertain about who was with her and where they were. She could hear nothing outside of the office except for Lily's coughs. There were countless ways this could go wrong, leading to harm for Lily.

Before leaving the room, Jonatan glanced at her door. With his right hand, he reached into the breast pocket of his vest, pulled out a set of keys, and jingled them before crossing the threshold and shutting the door behind him.

The click of the lock broke Bea. She clamped her hand over her mouth as sobs wracked her body. Help was just beyond the door, yet calling out posed too much risk. Bea could not allow Lily to endure the same fate that she might soon face.

THE SUN ROSE. THE sun set. Bea watched both every day through the hole in the wall; those were her only markers of time. She repeatedly asked Jonatan for the time or date, but his reply was always philosophical: "Time is irrelevant for you, clutched as you are, in the hands of education."

Often, he'd muse to her about how honored she should feel to have the opportunity to be trained by him. "You're learning the ways of medicine and anatomy free of charge from Bellview Hospital Medical College's top student." Then, he'd chuckle at his own joke.

Bea would feign a smile as she stood next to him, observing his autopsies. He didn't yet trust her to take his notes.

She kept track of the days by carving grooves in the wood above her mattress with a spoon. This morning, she carved the twentieth line. She'd only had the idea to start this twenty days ago, as her imprisonment was, well, traumatic, to say the least. Who knew how many days she had actually been here before she began to keep tally?

Bea began to accept her fate. No one was coming to save her. No one knew that she was even here. All the lies and webs of deceit that she'd woven across the United States covered her tracks well.

Jonatan made an incision beneath the clavicle of a new body. Raven-haired, just like her mother. Bea reached out with her left hand and twisted the locks between her fingers before raising her right hand to her chest. She had learned about the bones in the chest yesterday.

As Jonatan drew his knife—no bistoury—down the flesh of the sternum, a dark red line that bled trailed the blade. For the first time since running away, Bea wished her father knew where she was and would come to get her. Whatever punishment she received from him would be worlds better than what she was currently experiencing. This woman's hair, Bea twisted the locks tighter around her finger, so much like her mother's.

"Are you listening to me?" Jonatan glared up at her, both hands' index and middle fingers deftly placed in the incision, spreading the pale, blood-spotted flesh apart to expose the iridescent muscle underneath.

Bea shook her head, and the whoosh of an uncontrolled exhalation from her lungs jolted her. She hadn't realized she'd been holding her breath.

"What am I doing?" he asked again.

The rough lick of her tongue failed to provide any moisture to her lips. They cracked as she opened her mouth to speak. "You're, um…" she couldn't find the words.

The woman's ashen skin made Bea clasp her own hand to feel the warmth of life flowing through her veins. Her gaze drifted away from the ugly cut carved into the flesh, across the woman's indecently exposed breasts, to the deep gash across her throat—just like the other two women. All three had been killed in the same manner.

The blood rushed from her head as she looked upon the woman's face—eyes wide open in a cold, dead stare. Her pupils were nearly the size of a dime, so large that Bea couldn't tell the color of her iris. Bea wanted to rub her fingers over the woman's purplish-blue lips to give her some of her own warmth. It was all so unnatural.

"Bea!" Jonatan slammed his hand down on the counter behind them—the one now covered with a plethora of anatomy and medical books he'd brought into the office from his library to provide Bea the opportunity to study whenever she was alone, that is, alone without Jonatan. She was hardly ever truly alone.

He gently laid the tortoiseshell bistoury down on the metal stand next to the autopsy table; anger glinted in his eyes.

Bea stepped back, the heavy chain still locked around her right ankle, making its familiar dragging sound as she moved.

"I am spending my precious time trying to teach you the ways of medicine and you refuse to pay attention.

"No... I am trying to pay attention. It's just," she paused and looked at the partially flayed woman. She started to cry. "It's just so much death."

The hardened look in Jonatan's eyes remained as he picked up a scalpel that lay next to his prized bistoury. He slid the side table that held his instruments aside and stomped toward her. She stood frozen in place, unsure of what he was about to do.

Bea cried out, her voice shattered the thick silence of the room when he roughly grabbed her shoulder. The room spun at the thought of the scalpel in Jonatan's hand coolly slicing through the layers of skin across her throat.

He wrenched her arm, causing her to fall forward toward him. He stooped to look her in the eye. "Get ahold of yourself." He let go of her arm, grabbed her left hand, and slapped the handle of the scalpel into her palm.

"Open. Her. Up." He seethed.

"No...," she whispered.

The light hanging above the dead woman's body seemed to intensify. Bea closed her eyes against the throbbing in her head. She couldn't. She could not touch this woman.

"Do it."

Silence fell around Bea as she opened her eyes. A tingling numbness spread from her core to her extremities.

Bea thought back to her time traveling across the United States. Back to when she had to sleep with all those men for money. With each instance, she pushed aside her thoughts about *what* she was doing and focused on *why* she was doing it: food, a warm bed, and escape.

The secret is to keep breathing, she told herself as the edges of her vision blurred. A woman must do whatever it takes to keep going—to keep breathing.

The body before her drifted away, as though she were looking at the woman through the lens of a microscope. Bea felt her body move; it floated closer to the woman's body on its own accord out of sheer instinct for survival.

Ignoring the chest incision that Jonatan made, the tip of the scalpel slipped easily through the flesh in the soft spot beneath the lower tip of the breastbone. The flesh felt cold and rubbery as the scalpel separated the skin, straight down to the top of the pubic bone. The only area where additional pressure of the blade was needed was cutting through the tightly wadded skin of the woman's belly button. The umbilicus, as Jonatan calls it.

A horizontal line was drawn with the blade between the lower ribs, cutting across the vertical line that divided the abdomen. Then the flesh and muscle between the points of the hip bones were connected by another bisecting horizontal line.

Once the scalpel was done cutting, a capital letter "I" was engraved on the corpse's abdomen. Following the "I" pattern, the scalpel reflected the tissue with each slight pass to cut through each individual layer of flesh. The gentle teasing of each layer prevented the internal organs from being prematurely perforated during the incision. Then, the two flaps of flesh were peeled back like the pages of a book, and the internal viscera of the corpse were exposed.

Fingers slipped through the slick gossamer that bound the organs in place. Intestines were uncoiled by hands that found the texture to be firm as they pulled and rolled the organ between the fingertips. As the entrails were removed and piled in a rope-like heap on top of the corpse's pubic area, larger hands grasped onto the smaller working ones and pulled them away from the corpse.

"That's enough," a male's voice said.

Bea's vision came sharply back in focus to find Jonatan clutching her bloody hands between his own over top of the woman's body. Bea looked down at the exposed abdomen, the viscera iridescent under the dancing flicker of the kerosene lamps.

She wondered whether they would find what Jonatan was seeking: proof that women were inherently sinful. Could he be right? Was this her punishment for the sins she had committed herself?

"*One of us.*" A voice hissed. Bea turned her attention to the dead woman's face, which remained unchanged. A hard lump in Bea's throat throbbed up and down her windpipe as she attempted to speak, but all she could manage were soft squeaks.

"That's enough for today." Still holding her hands, Jonatan walked around the table, pivoting Bea with his movement and guiding her to the washbasin. He plunged her hands into the already brownish-red, tainted cool water and washed the blood from her hands.

"I-I-I-I," Bea's mouth moved, but she couldn't articulate her lips to form words—words that she was even struggling to form in her mind. She couldn't fathom what had happened. One moment, Jonatan put the scalpel in her hand; the next, her hands were deep inside the woman's body.

"I-I-I-I," Bea continued to sputter.

"I'm very proud of you. An excellent cut, albeit it's a bit jagged and haphazard. We'll work on that." Jonatan dried her hands and led her back to the little room. The cuff around Bea's ankle bit into her skin as the chain dragged behind her, following in her footsteps. Every sensation on her skin was amplified.

The shaking started the moment she set foot inside the closet. Jonatan didn't light her lamp but instead pushed the chain the rest of the way into the room behind her and closed the door, plunging Bea into darkness.

"I-I-I-I," was all she could say to the closed door. After several moments of rustling from the other side of the door, the light seeping into the closet from beneath it vanished. The sound of another door closing echoed in her mind.

The lump in Bea's throat eased, and a scream tore from her lips. When she ran out of breath, she crumpled onto the mattress behind her on the floor.

"*One of us. One of us,*" the voice whispered from the other room.

The sound of the other door closing signaled Jonatan's departure. Bea knew the woman was the only other person left in that room.

Bea sobbed as she fell onto her back on the mattress. Struggling to stop her shaking, she pulled the quilt over her body.

For the first time in twenty days, Bea didn't look through the hole in the wall to watch the sunset. Instead, she remained on the mattress and listened to the haunting, soft whispers of the woman in the other room repeating: *One of us.*

Chapter 9

THE SECRET IS TO KEEP BREATHING

THE SUN HAD NOT yet cast its first rays above the prairie's horizon, but a golden, bluish-purple haze swirled before the coming dawn. Bea had not slept that night. Every time she closed her eyes, she saw her hands buried deep within the woman's abdomen, digging around as if she were searching for something. Darkness enclosed them, but she knew Jonatan stood just beyond her line of sight. She could hear him breathing, occasionally interrupted by a cough.

"*Keep digging, keep digging.*" The woman—flat on her back atop the autopsy table, had her head lifted while she whispered encouragement to Bea. Cold and dead, her eyes looked straight forward past her open abdominal cavity and Bea. Her mouth remained shut, though her encouraging words kept flowing.

The murk and muck of the woman's insides were warm and silken. Bea's hands swam effortlessly in and around the woman's organs, groping, squeezing, and pinching—feeling for the texture of something hard and round—like a pearl—a beautiful opalescent sphere floating amongst waves of viscera.

"Nothing's there, nothing's there."

Bea never found what Jonatan had her searching for. She'd been buried nearly up to her shoulders when Jonatan stepped out of the darkness in front of her.

His face showed no emotion as he raised his prized bistoury in his right hand. His neck cracked as his head tilted to the left, ear meeting his shoulder.

A crazed, thin, wide smile broke through his mask. "Find it yet?"

"No." Bea couldn't steady the tremor in her voice.

"That's because it's in you." Jonatan struck forward with the scalpel toward Bea's neck.

But before any contact was made, she jolted awake. That same dream invaded every moment she had tried to fall asleep that night. Well before sunrise, she climbed off her mattress, wrapped herself in the quilt, and tried not to think about what lay in the next room. She slid aside the slat that covered the hole to the outside and stared into the darkness.

Behind the darkness of the new moon, stars shone brightly, cascading across the vast sky through Bea's secluded view. The twinkling stars and delicate wisps of distant clouds beckoned her to fly. If only she could escape this place, she would soar from this world just as Lily described when they lay on the prairie grass together. She longed to spread her arms wide and urge the wind to swirl around her, lifting her high and far away from here.

The circumference of her view was confined. The peculiar thickness of the wall gave her porthole a tubular visual effect, as if she'd have to navigate through an endless tunnel before reaching her freedom at the end. The wall's thickness seemed as deep as her forearm—not typical for a home in this area. Bea wondered about the other room—the one outside the room where the woman lay. It had been a while since she'd been outside Jonatan's office, and details about the rest of his house were fuzzy in her memory. Were the walls in the rest of the house as thick as these?

Bea continued to stare outside, willing the sun to rise so she could see the clear blue sky of a new day. She picked at a splinter next to the hole to distract herself from thinking she might have been here for more than the twenty ticks she'd marked on the wall. She could be going on two months... or more.

"Don't think of things you don't want answers to."

The voice was still not her own. Bea was coming to terms with the fact that these dead women were talking—and only speaking to her. She kept her focus on the outside as she listened to the woman speaking loudly enough to make it through the closed door. That woman was right. Bea shouldn't dwell on such things—things that she didn't want answers to.

While the sun itself hid behind the wall to her right, Bea marveled at the dawn's rainbow in the changing sky. The kaleidoscope of colors soon faded into a bright blue early morning. Birds chirped and sang as they darted through the calf-high grass, catching whatever tiny insects they could spot.

The thing she missed most about the East Coast was the abundance of trees. While the Colorado prairies were beautiful, they felt foreign to the nature she was accustomed to—despite growing up in the city. Her family had a summer home just outside of the city. A small chateau-like property tucked away among the trees.

Even though Bea was young the last time she visited during the summer before her mother became ill, she could still recall all the woodland sounds: the feel of the damp, mossy earth beneath her toes as she played in the woods, and the taste of rustic, piney warmth as she breathed in deeply. Amid those trees was where she felt she belonged.

In the West, she felt like an outsider—someone everyone should be wary of. She didn't belong.

For the first time in her life, Bea felt a sense of homesickness. A void of emptiness and loneliness formed in her chest. She missed the trees. But she could never go home; given her current situation, she'd never have a chance, even if she wanted to.

From the other side of her door, she heard a rattle. Bea turned away from her little window and cautiously stepped toward the door. Not sure of what was making the sound, she knelt and looked through the little hole.

The door in the other room was open, allowing light to filter in. Jonatan entered, carrying a tray, and set it down on the counter behind the woman as he reached for the hanging lamp above the body. Bea shrank back from the hole as a brighter light filled the room. Once her eyes adjusted, she turned to see Jonatan pulling the sheet off the woman's body.

Bea's legs trembled; she wanted to run but remained steadfast, watching. While she couldn't clearly see what he was looking at from her spot, she didn't miss the deepening frown on his face. Then he stuck his hand inside the woman, prompting Bea to look off to the left. That's when she noticed the door outside the woman's room was still open.

Through the doorway, Bea noticed the library's front window wide open, letting in the fresh outdoor air. The thin off-white curtain fluttered in the breeze. Flashes of blue sky sparkled beyond the glass pane. The seat and right arm of the rocking chair were also visible, along with the end table and the usual stack of books. Bea longed to sit once more in that chair and inhale the fresh air.

A huff brought her attention back to Jonatan as he covered the body and tucked the sheet around the woman. Bea had never seen him do that before. He then closed the office door, severing Bea's connection with the open window. She closed her eyes, feeling like she'd just been locked away again.

She slid back across the wooden floor and pulled her pants-clad knees to her chin. She buried her nose in the fabric, trying to subdue the scream that scratched to be released from her throat.

He opened the closet door and entered with a tray of breakfast. On the plate were eggs, bacon, coffee, and water. No words were exchanged between them as he set the tray down before her and lit the room's lamp before returning to the woman's body. He left the closet door open, perhaps assuming she'd emerge after finishing her breakfast.

The meaty, fatty smell of the bacon stirred a deep hunger in Bea, and she scrambled forward. She couldn't remember the last time she had bacon. Up until this point, she'd only been fed soup or broth. The aroma was intoxicating. The meat glistened as she held a single strip up to the light. The off-white, marbled with pink pork flesh reminded her of the woman's stomach muscle. Bea's abdomen clenched at the thought. Acidic, hot bile surged up her throat, but she quickly swallowed, not knowing where to deposit it.

The meal in front of her was a masterpiece compared to the usual congealed soup. But she couldn't stomach it. She set the ration of meat aside, sliding the tray out of her direct line of sight.

Outside the room, she watched Jonatan tuck and tie the sheet around the body.

"What are you doing?" she asked.

He wiped his brow. Since he'd entered, the room had grown stuffy. Bea could feel the atmosphere of that room encroaching on her own.

"She's going to be buried. We didn't find what we were looking for." He tied the two corners of the sheet in a knot above the woman's chest.

"We?" Bea whispered.

Jonatan stood up straight and looked at the wrapped body before him. "I'll be gone for the night, but will leave you with dinner and breakfast." He glanced at her, then at the barely touched tray beside her. "Or maybe I'll leave that for you to eat as your next few meals." A hint of anger tinged his voice.

Bea he knew he'd taken the time to cook a meal for her, and she was letting it go to waste. "I need to walk and stretch a bit before I eat. I'll eat in a moment." She lied. Deep down, she knew *that* food would never pass her lips. The bacon reminded her too much of human flesh, leaving her without hunger. But her response seemed to be one that satisfied him.

"I'll be right back." He opened the door to the other room

Bea's attention immediately snapped to the open door and the window beyond. She paid no mind to Jonatan as he picked up the woman and carried her out of the room. He left the door open as he disappeared into the rest of the house.

Losing all fear, Bea stood and took tentative steps out of the closet and into Jonatan's office. Just a few more steps, and she could run—she could be free.

The chain behind her rattled as she moved forward, reminding her that she was trapped.

She breathed deeply and continued walking forward despite the chain. If there was a way she could remove it...

The key. Both the office and shackle keys were probably still in his vest pocket. And as always, he wore that same vest day in and day out—an idea formed in her mind. Jonatan's vest was starting to look a little tattered.

She padded over to the dining table and chairs on her left, quietly slid out the chair closest to the open door, and sat, waiting for Jonatan to return.

He jumped as he rounded the corner. Their eyes locked, and the lie that Bea was about to tell solidified in her mind. "What are you doing?" His voice faltered despite an attempt to sound firm.

"Just enjoying the fresh breeze from the window." She smiled and leaned back further in her seat to signal that she was comfortable. "Where are you heading off to later?"

He looked at her, and the slightly puzzled expression on his face disappeared. "Denver City."

"And is that the outfit you're wearing?"

"It is."

She chuckled. "You can't go into the city with a vest that looks that tattered."

Jonatan looked down and fingered a hole beginning to form near his collar. "I don't have another one."

"How about you leave that here with me to mend while you get ready for your trip?" The smile on her face never faltered.

However, Jonatan seemed to hesitate at her answer, perhaps trying to figure out how to proceed. After a moment, he turned to the cabinet on the opposite side of the room from Bea. Amid all his medical and surgical equipment, Jonatan retrieved a needle and thread. Then he removed his vest. A spasm of coughs wracked him. Bea persuaded herself to appear concerned. She got up and reached for him. He drew away slightly before placing the vest in her extended hand, followed by the needle and thread.

"Actually, I was going to lie down for a few moments, as I don't feel the best after moving the last test subject." Jonatan never said what he did with the women's bodies, nor was Bea about to ask. She sat down to inspect the holes in his vest, purposefully ignoring the breast pockets.

"Thank you," Jonatan said as he moved to the door.

"Wait!" she said as he began to close the door on her.

He stopped and glared at her.

"I'm not going anywhere." She nodded at her leg, where the chain still sat attached. "Could you leave it open so I can enjoy the breeze and the view while I work? It's been so long since I've been able to see outside."

Jonatan stood there for a long moment, looking at the chain. Bea tried to catch his eye to distract him from dwelling on it for too long, lest he remember the keys. Once she escaped Jonatan's house, she'd run into town to find help.

"Just this once, and don't do anything irrational. Besides, if you escaped, you'd be dead. You'd never survive out on the prairie alone, and the moment you stepped into town..." He gave her no further explanation.

Bea gasped, losing control of her resolve. "What does that mean?"

His cold, thin smile mirrored the iciness of his eyes. "I have friends there who know me very well." And with that, he turned and disappeared from the room, leaving Bea next to the open door.

She waited until his footsteps faded around the corner and ascended the stairs. Bea focused her gaze on the open window, pushing Jonatan's threat to the back of her mind. Finding help in town was a chance she had to take. Her fingers moved nimbly across the black cotton fabric of Jonatan's vest. If he made any motion to return, she would most likely hear him coming down the stairs before she saw him round the corner. She felt for the keys in his breast pocket, holding her breath as her hands traversed—hoping the keys were really there. She had simply assumed he never removed them.

That assumption proved to be correct as the outline of a key formed under her fingertips beneath the fabric. Unable to restrain herself any longer, she dug them out and draped the vest over the chair's arm. Resting her foot on the seat, she pulled up the linen pant leg and inhaled sharply at the bruised, marred flesh around her ankle. The cuff had worn her skin raw.

Bea slid the key into the lock and attempted to turn it. The lock tumbler wouldn't budge. Beads of perspiration gathered at the back of her neck and down her back, a slight fear creeping in that maybe these were not the right keys. She removed the key from the shackle and tried the second one.

With a turn, the tumbler moved, and the lock clicked, the two halves of the shackle separating and exposing the flesh of her ankle for the first time in many months. Her skin was raw underneath, and she hadn't realized how painful it felt until she saw the wound. Tears welled in her eyes, but she took a long breath to steady herself.

"Just breathe," she said. "And run."

Quietly, she laid the shackle and chain on the floor, then tiptoed out of Jonatan's office. The short hallway led to the library. She had forgotten how many books Jonatan had lined the wall of bookshelves. She paused for a moment. *Had he gotten more?* And the layer of dust that had settled on the furniture—Jonatan had not been cleaning. No one had been cleaning all this time.

Go! Don't think, just go, she mentally chided herself. Bea leaned toward the door but thought better of it. She couldn't remember if the hinges squeaked when it opened. The window in front of her was wide open, the curtain billowing in the breeze and beckoning her forward. She ignored the thoughts about the filth that had accumulated since she had been locked away from cleaning. As quietly as she could, she climbed through the window onto the porch.

She started toward the dusty road leading into the prairie but stopped short after jumping off the porch. With a half-turn, she noticed the second-floor windows wide open, facing the road. Even though those were the windows to the loft where she used to sleep, she wasn't sure if Jonatan could see her through those or the two windows on the left side of the house that were in his bedroom. She ran to the right, where no second-floor windows looked out onto the prairie.

The dry, knee-high grass swished against her, with the shorter blades pricking at her feet. She tried to ignore the pain and willed her legs to move faster. The prairie stretched endlessly around her. Her breath raggedly tore from her mouth as a sharp sting pierced her side. Bea tumbled forward into the grass. Little crickets and other insects fled from her descent to avoid being crushed beneath her. She got up slowly, then craned her neck to look behind her toward where she had been imprisoned. In that direction, the mountains loomed far off in the distance. She swept her gaze across the mountain line and back toward where she currently sat. Along the way, shimmering in the distance, she could make out the outline of Yellow Creek City. It was far off, but still within walking distance.

But that was all.

There was nothing else around her. Nowhere else for her to go. Then there was the threat Jonatan had made about her returning to town. The threat solidified in her mind that the sheriff had played a role in her abduction. She couldn't go to him for help. And Bea wasn't sure who else knew about Jonatan's work. Her mind drifted to the woman from the boarding house who confronted the sheriff on the day she arrived in Yellow Creek City. That woman could help her!

Bea was suddenly urged to find her, but it was a blur when she tried to recall the woman's face. Questions swirled in her mind as she wondered if the woman was still in town. She had confronted the sheriff—almost threatening—about her missing girls, who were likely past subjects of Jonatan's. Bea feared that the woman may have ended up on Jonatan's table at some point during Bea's employment. She wasn't certain, but it would be too risky for Jonatan to allow someone like her to live—someone who raised questions and concerns about missing girls.

The sun climbed into the sky, indicating it was still morning. She didn't know when the next train would arrive, nor did she have any money to buy a ticket, leaving her vulnerable to capture. A soft sob escaped Bea's lips as she lay back in the grass.

"Please, God. Just let me pass into the dirt." Tears flowed, and her lips cracked with thirst. The morning heat beat down on her, threatening to intensify as the day wore on. She needed water and thought back to the tray of food, coffee, and water in her room. *Her room.*

A sea of endless blue stretched far beyond the prairie grass that danced in her periphery. A warm 'shhhhh' enveloped her as the winds blew through the grass, making the tall blades dance, alive and rejoicing in the sun. The world hummed beneath her, breathing and pulsating against her back. Bea prayed that she could become one with the Earth. Her life was nothing but pain and running. She belonged nowhere, and yet, in this moment, she felt connected to everywhere. But she couldn't stay here, not in this spot. She had to decide.

Bea sat up and sniffed before wiping her nose with the back of her hand. Even though Jonatan held her captive against her will, he took care of her. No man—not even her father—had ever cared for her.

Jonatan provided her with what she needed to survive: a safe place to sleep and warm meals. He offered her security so she wouldn't have to continue working in the same dangerous way she had been to make money. It never once crossed Bea's mind that Jonatan would take advantage of her. In fact, he never propositioned her—never even looked at her in a way that suggested desire.

For that, Bea was genuinely grateful. She had never taken pleasure in intimacy and couldn't imagine feeling that way toward Jonatan. Her experiences with the act of pleasure had always been transactional, a means to an end, and she had never felt any emotional pull or physical longing for the men she had dealt with. In truth, she couldn't recall ever feeling attracted to anyone.

With Jonatan, the absence of desire felt like safety. Even with the other women he brought into her room, he treated them with the same lack of desire. The only difference with them was that he was more clinical and detached, treating them more like subjects and nothing more. Additionally, while in Jonatan's care, Bea has received an education far beyond anything she had previously experienced. Never in her lifetime did she expect to receive formal instruction on the workings of the human body. All that was asked of her in return was to learn and assist Jonatan with his research—work that she disagreed with and considered immoral. However, she had to do what was necessary to survive.

Bea turned her gaze back to the mountain range behind her—toward the direction of San Francisco. What did she have there? Bea didn't know. At that moment, she was penniless and without her belongings. If she ran and made it to that city, she would be homeless. How could she even get there without a train ticket and any money? Her belongings were lost to her. If they still existed, they were at Jonatan's house. Everything she had—everything that she needed—was back in his house. She turned her gaze to the structure she had just escaped.

The two-story house stood tall amid the prairie grass. Slatted wood siding and dark blue painted shutters caught her eye. She had never paid much attention to the appearance of his house before. From where Bea sat, the shingled roof looked somewhat new, but what did she really know about architecture? What she did know was that it was a solid, sturdy house.

Running out west left her unfamiliar with San Francisco, with nothing but the clothes on her back and uncertainty about how she would reach her destination.

"The secret is to keep breathing," Bea said as she rose and turned back toward Jonatan's home.

Chapter 10

THE SKY LOOKED SO BLUE

B EA FOUND PEACE IN her daily routine. Her small window through the old chimney pipe hole, which Jonatan had confirmed to be accurate, dictated her time of day. She conditioned herself to wake before the sun rose each morning with a full-body stretch. Then she slid the little board out of the way to watch the dawn colors transform into beautiful blue mornings. Before going to bed, if she made it in time, she watched the colors of dusk shift into darkness.

Jonatan stopped locking the door between her room and the office, granting her free rein over both spaces. He left all his medical books and journals on the counter in his office and gave Bea her own journal as well. She spent much of her days reading and taking notes in it. The women Jonatan brought home became sporadic, and he was gone for longer periods of time between them. Bea sensed he had to travel further away to find new specimens. While she didn't like being alone, she was starting to enjoy her solitude more for studying.

Despite Jonatan becoming increasingly irritable, he still took care of her, ensuring she had enough supplies while he was gone—food, water, and rags for when her menstrual cycle arrived. He trusted her with matches and extra metal containers of kerosene to keep her lamps lit. He'd also made her a toilet from an old barrel lined with a waterproof tarp, which was an improvement over the chamber pot.

Bea hated it when he was away for more than three days. The rooms became stuffy, and the barrel started to smell. At least when Jonatan was home and in the office with her, he sometimes left the locked door to the rest of the house open, letting in fresh air. The women tended to smell after a day or two.

This morning, Bea woke up with a cramp in her leg. Instead of her morning stretch and looking through her little window, she started with a walk. Halfway around the autopsy table, then a turn, and finish with a half-circle the other way.

"Do you think it's a nice morning today?" Bea asked the woman on the table.

The woman's hair was a deep, rich chestnut like Bea's, but where Bea had beautiful curls, this woman's hair was thin and straight.

"I have a bit of a pain in my leg. Think I must have slept on it funny." She continued her half-circles around the table. "It's starting to feel better, though."

Bea yawned and stretched. Her stomach growled. "I hope Jonatan comes soon. I'm getting hungry."

She stood near the woman's head, gently raking her fingers through her hair, combing out any knots, and making it look soft and smooth. Then, she adjusted the sheet to cover the body so that the top lined up just below the woman's jawline. She did this to conceal the gash across the throat and to hide the dissected midsection. The woman would be gone from here today and replaced with another.

"Before you go later, where are you from?" She smoothed out the creases in the sheet. Despite being dead, Bea wanted the woman to be comfortable before she left. "I guess you're the silent type," she mused, feeling a bit dejected that this one hadn't spoken to her. It wasn't like the others really spoke with her much, either. They'd say a word or two that caused Bea to feel fearful at first, as they seemed to insinuate that Bea was just like them and likely to be next on the table.

Upon first hearing the voices, she thought she was losing her sanity and began to worry that she might be haunted. But lately, she had given up on overthinking it, welcoming the feminine voices when they appeared and missing them when they were absent—even though they didn't really say much to her to begin with. There was a comfort in their few words.

"Let's go see if it's morning yet." Bea shuffled back into her small room, her chain dragging behind her. There was a slight tug as she crossed the threshold of her door. She turned to pick up the chain, which had caught on the leg of the autopsy table. Bending down to lift it, she looked at the worn marks on the floor from many weeks of walking. After her last attempt, Bea had never tried to escape again.

Since that day, she'd stopped marking the passing of days on the wall with the spoon she still had hidden under her mattress. She'd given up caring because Bea realized and accepted there was nowhere she could go where she'd be safe. This was the safest place she had been since her mother passed, and her father revealed his true motives.

He had never wanted a daughter; what he had was a servant who could maintain the house—free of charge.

With the chain brought back into her room, Bea slid the board to her small window. When she moved it this time, it wobbled slightly. As she wiggled the board to figure out what was wrong, the nail securing it to the wall snapped in half, causing the board to fall from the wall and Bea's fingertips, landing with a cracking thud on her toes. Bea screamed and jumped back, holding her right foot in the air as pain shot across the top of her foot and up her shin. The skin beneath her big toe's toenail turned purple in the dim light of her kerosene lamp.

When she tried to put her foot back on the floor, the weight on her toe caused excruciating pain. The office door flew open, and Jonatan rushed in. Bea, standing one-legged, turned to see a concerned Jonatan walking toward her. She spread her hand over the open hole, fingers splayed, attempting to hide her little window.

"What's going on?" He looked directly at her, not noticing the exposed hole. She let go of the wall and hopped over to him, maintaining eye contact. With a slight raise of her leg, she directed his attention to her foot. Any look of concern evaporated as he bent over and took her foot into his hand. She knew he was slipping into his "doctor" frame of mind.

"What happened?" he asked.

"I...um..." she fumbled for the words, not wanting to reveal the truth. He looked up at her, then past her.

"What is that?" his voice deepened. He let go of her foot, pushed past her, and walked up to the wall. He fingered the edge of the hole.

"Um, the board that covered that old chimney hole fell on my foot." She tried to direct him to look at her foot again.

"How did it fall?"

"I bumped it, and it fell."

He ignored her foot, fixating his focus on the hole. "The nail is worn and snapped in half. Something like this doesn't just *fall*."

"I... I'm sorry. I move it every morning and evening to watch the sun rise and set. It's how I get an idea of what time it is."

"Looking outside?" He then muttered something quietly to himself and ran his hand over the hole before turning to her. "Are you looking to escape?"

"No, Jonatan!" She said.

"If you were content here with me, you would not need to look outside to tell the time. Time is irrelevant to you!" He towered over her. Bea shivered at the heat that seemed to radiate from his body and consume her. "I trusted you. And you want to leave me!"

"Wha—How could you...why would you think that?" She reached for him, but he stormed past her. Bea tried to chase after him, but the moment she stepped, pain from her toe shot up her foot and leg.

She collapsed back onto her bed, foot in hand, and cried. As she wept, Bea tried to understand what she did wrong. All she wanted was to look outside. Just to see something other than the inside of these rooms and the bodies they contain.

Shuffling and banging came from the other side of the wall behind Bea, followed by sawing. She hobbled to her feet. Looking through the hole, she saw nothing, and then

Jonatan's face appeared. He glowered at her before something covered the hole, which was followed by hammering. Lots of hammering.

Bea stared into the darkness. Her small window to the outside world was now shut, and all she could see was an endless night. She raised her hand to the hole, and for the first time, she pushed her hand inside and moved forward—only to be met by something solid and unyielding. Jonatan had nailed up a new board, one on the outside of the house. One that she could no longer move.

When he returned, he left the office door wide open. Bea shrank back as his face was red and dripping with sweat. He walked over to the dining table and fell forward, grasping the edge before a coughing fit exploded from his mouth.

Bea made no move to support him or check if he was okay.

He approached the woman and wrapped her up by tying two corners together above her breast. This time, he struggled and wheezed as he picked her up, but he was able to steady himself and carry her out. Bea slipped out of her room, the ever-persistent chain dragging behind her, into the space between the dining and autopsy tables.

The pain in her toe had begun to subside, indicating that it was most likely not broken. However, it was still tender, and she'd probably lose the nail. The purpling in her nail bed was becoming darker. Reflecting on Jonatan's lack of empathy toward her, she gazed out the open office door at the prairie framed by the library window.

But that only lasted a few moments because Jonatan was back with another woman. Bea stepped back as he came in and put the body on the autopsy table.

"Get started." He nodded to the woman as he readjusted his vest before closing the office door, trapping all three of them in this room together. Pushing past the lingering pain in her toe, she shuffled to the table and began removing the woman's clothes and undergarments. There was once a time when this made her uncomfortable. Then she started to enjoy it because she missed touching the fabric of dresses and lace. Today, however, touching the dress felt like nothing more than ordinary cloth beneath her fingertips. She didn't even care to notice what kind of fabric the dress was made of.

Bea was working on the front of the woman's dress when she noticed that her throat wasn't cut. This one had died differently. There was bruising on the neck, but no cuts. Her mouth went dry, yet she continued to remove the woman's clothes. Something was changing. Jonatan was short with her—seemingly annoyed most of the time. He was also coughing more frequently; perhaps he was sick.

Bea put the dress and undergarments into the refuse can in the back corner of the room and thought nothing more about how this woman died.

Jonatan readied his instruments as Bea took her seat at the dining table. Before her lay an open journal with blank pages and a pen. She placed the nib pen down next to the inkwell. This journal, along with the stack of journals against the wall before her, was filled with her beautiful cursive script and illustrations. She tried her best to write down everything Jonatan said as he performed his autopsies, and she mostly captured it all. Despite berating her for her occasional misspellings, he seemed pleased with her notetaking. Even more so, he was quite impressed with her sketches. At one point, he even brought her colored pencils to brighten them up.

"Another body of sin is gone," Jonatan said, "sent to be with her hellish master."

The side of Bea's pinky smudged the last sentence she'd written as she began to shake. The knowledge that she was full of sin resurfaced in her mind. She had done things—the same things that these women had once done. Jonatan still didn't know. And if he ever found out...

Looking at the woman's neck, Bea felt compelled to try a different approach with Jonatan. She sensed that things were starting to change with him, and not for the better. She needed to get to the bottom of what was going on.

"Jonatan?"

"Hmm?"

"Maybe these women sell themselves to make a living wage to survive. They—"

"Preposterous!" he shouted at her. "There are many ways to make money. Finding a husband for a start would ease that burden."

Bea wanted to argue with him more but decided against it for fear of revealing herself. She adjusted the shackle around her ankle out of nervousness and then changed the subject. "All this time I've been documenting these autopsies, you've never explained how they are...," she slid her finger across her throat, "Shouldn't that method be documented as well?"

Jonatan stood and adjusted the apron around his neck and waist. At one time, the apron might've been a pristine white. Now, it was yellowish and coated with a variety of stains. "The one who is dispatching these women is quite intelligent. One of the most silent and quick ways to dispatch someone is by cutting the main blood supply to the brain." He picked up his bistoury and pointed to an intact point on the woman's neck. "See here? This is where one of the carotid arteries runs. There's another in the same place on the other side of the neck."

Bea looked at the bruises on this woman's neck.

"Cut one carotid, and a person bleeds out in fifteen seconds. Cut the second, and it's half that time." He smiled. "The two points are connected to open the throat, releasing the sinful breath out of the body."

"But not this one?" Bea asked. "She's not cut. Why?" She had long realized that Jonatan was the one murdering these women, but she never outright asked him about it. However, after his actions today in closing off her view of the outside world—the only view that she had control over—Bea felt as though she had nothing else left to lose.

He didn't immediately answer; he just stared at the woman before him. At that moment, his face changed. It softened, and the atmosphere in the room shifted, becoming lighter. "I've been having bad dreams lately."

Bea gasped. "You've been having bad dreams?"

Balling up his fists, he raised one to his lips and coughed. Swallowing hard, he continued, "I've been dreaming of my mother. This one. She looks like my mother."

The woman had long, straight black hair. "Your mother?" Bea asked. "Is she back in New York with your father?"

Jonatan scowled before covering his mouth again as an explosive coughing fit erupted from him. Once finished, he removed his hand, smearing bright red blood across his lips.

Bea stood to assist him.

"Sit down!" He glared at her, licked his lips, and wiped his bloody hand on his apron. Bea didn't move and continued to stand. He sighed and took the chair across the table from her. He laid his bistoury knife on the table.

"You and I have been together for some time. And I consider you a friend." He shook his head and was silent for a moment before looking up at her. "My mother was a whore; despite being married to my father."

Bea didn't react and maintained eye contact with him. He picked up his bistoury and held it between both hands.

"They were childless until one day when my mother became pregnant. My father claimed that it shouldn't have been possible for him to impregnate her due to a childhood accident he experienced. But who really knows? I could be my father's child or someone else's. My father resented her from the moment she found out. She died while giving birth to me, but not before trying to kill me herself. My father told me that she tried to deliver me with the umbilical cord wrapped around my neck when I was born, nearly choking me to death. He saved me by cutting me and the cord out of her."

Bea was silent for a moment, now understanding the motivation behind Jonatan's hypothesis and research. Despite being at risk of finding herself at the end of his knife, warmth enveloped her. She felt sympathy for him. His own mother—a parent—had tried to kill him. They shared something in common. And Bea couldn't shake the urge to reveal their connection, even though she had worked so hard to conceal her past. Perhaps she could share a bit with him. It could help re-establish their dwindling bond. She wanted to solidify with him that she is a friend.

"My father tried to kill me. My family is wealthy; my father owns a mining company, and I grew up in Philadelphia. He was a hateful and distant man. My mother was the exact opposite. She's the one who taught me how to read, write, and draw. She died from consumption when I was seven. My father spiraled and turned to alcohol and gambling. With his finances dwindling because of his habits, he let go of all the staff and forced me to manage the household."

Jonatan just stared; no reaction or emotion crossed his face.

"Why pay staff when a person who lives in the house can care for it for free?" Bea sat down in her seat. "I lived as his servant for thirteen years until I dropped a glass one night, and it shattered on the kitchen floor. He beat me within an inch of my life with his fists. The next morning, while he was sleeping, I packed a bag with all the clothes I could fit and took two hundred from his office. I caught the first train to Pittsburgh. After I found out that he'd sent men after me, I continued further west. I've been making it on my own ever since."

That was too much. She bit her lip to keep her mouth shut. She'd revealed too much.

Jonatan stood, walked to the other side of the woman on the table, and placed his tortoiseshell bistoury alongside his other surgical tools on the smaller table next to the autopsy table. Their eyes met, and for the first time, Bea thought he saw her, not her secret. She carried a lot of pain, which meant she had to make it on her own.

"It's awful, what you went through." He sounded sincere. "Despite my father not knowing if I was his own, he treated me well and supported me. He was a man of science and God. He believed there was a reason that I lived, besides his intervention." Jonatan gestured to the body before them. "This is my reason."

He picked up the bistoury knife and ran a finger over the back curve of the blade and down the handle before placing his hand on the woman's intact chest. The dreams of his mother had affected him in such a way that they changed his approach to how he handled this woman. Bea knew he'd found her a few days ago, as the woman was in decay. She didn't understand why he hadn't brought the woman to this room sooner. Not that it mattered to her; Jonatan had his reasons. And the odor didn't bother her either. She'd grown used to the smell of death.

Jonatan started by conducting a thorough external exam of the body. After searching her hair and inspecting her orifices, he began the dissection. But instead of cutting her chest and abdomen open, he started on her right breast. Although Bea couldn't see what he was doing from that angle because Jonatan was blocking her view, she attempted to write down everything he dictated.

He walked around the body, faced in Bea's direction, and turned his attention to the underside of her right breast. He continued the incision by pulling his bistoury toward the sternum, then began to tease away the skin—exposing a globby yellow substance and white tissue. Bea placed her hand on her own breast.

"Did you hear me?" Jonatan said, looking up from the woman's chest.

Bea snapped to attention and mumbled, "I'm sorry. I missed what you said."

He repeated, his tone laced with annoyance, what he had found while cutting open the breast: nothing but fat, tissue, muscle, and ductwork. The incision was repeated on the left breast, once more revealing nothing unusual.

He set down his bistoury and sighed. "Nothing out of the ordinary." He mumbled and approached a washbasin on the countertop behind him and, with rough motions, washed the dead woman's muck off his hands. Disappointment radiated from him. "I'll make us dinner."

He took off his apron, hung it on a hook on the back of the door, and left.

"I'm sorry if you were treated poorly before he brought you here. I do hope he was respectful," Bea said to the woman, trying not to think about why Jonatan had waited so long before bringing her here. "No, he would be respectful. Jonatan isn't that kind of man. He's not like the others…"

"You need to stop talking to him," the woman on the table said. "You'll be caught."

Bea jumped from her seat. The woman's head rolled to the side, her pale blue and bloodshot eyes fixed on her. "Stop getting close to him. He's becoming unhinged."

"You're… you're talking to me." Bea was shocked. This woman wasn't just making brief statements to her like the others did when they spoke. This one was engaging in full conversation.

"Have you given up on escape?"

"W-w-what?" Bea shivered; the room felt like an icebox.

"You know he'll never let you go."

"Would that be so bad? I'm taken care of here."

"Until he finds out what kind of woman you are. Then you'll be in my place."

"Stop it." Bea covered her eyes and willed the woman to be silent.

"You know he won't find what he's looking for. The problem isn't us, but men. They are the ones who push us into situations where we must sell ourselves to survive."

Bea lowered her hands. "My father caused my problems."

"Mine did the same," said the woman.

"What's your name?" Bea asked.

The woman didn't respond.

"My name is Bea."

The woman's hazy eyes stayed locked on Bea, never blinking. "I... I don't remember my name."

Bea averted her gaze to her hands in her lap. How terrible it is to forget your own name. No one should be without a name. "I know," Bea said. "Let's call you Emily."

"Emily," the woman said. The name drifted in the air.

"Yes...um, it was my mother's name." Bea returned her gaze to the woman, who still hadn't moved.

"It's a nice name," said the woman.

A smile cracked across Bea's face. A real smile. One that she felt she hadn't displayed since her mother had passed. She was happy to have her mother's name said once again.

A wave of dizziness washed over Bea as the threads of reality spun around her, plucked as if she were trapped in a spider's web—and the spider delicately stepped toward her. Bea sighed.

"What's wrong?" Emily asked.

"Jonatan is my friend."

"You think that man is your friend?"

Bea chewed her lip. She had been with him for so long. At first, she trusted him—trusted him enough to come work for him. Then, after he imprisoned her in his office, she feared him and wanted nothing more than to escape. All the bodies had been too much. Yet he had shown her kindness, providing her with a safe place to live, food, and the stability she hadn't had since her mother was alive.

She wasn't keen on being imprisoned, and she disagreed with his research. These women were only doing what they needed to survive. Bea had to look beyond that and Jonatan's reasons. He brought her into his work, and she was learning human anatomy. Maybe one day, he'd allow her to help him in his medical practice outside of the room.

"Your silence tells me you don't believe that," Emily said.

"I don't agree with his work," Bea replied, "but he is teaching me,"

Emily snorted. "I'm glad my death—by the hands of your *friend*, no less—is helping your education."

Bea looked at the floor, where she had worn a path during her stay—a path carved by dragging her chain as she paced in boredom and shared her life with dead women. Emily was silent, her face turned up to the ceiling.

"The problem is within men," Emily said. "And deep down, you know that, too."

Emily wasn't wrong. It was only a matter of time before Bea was found out and suffered the same fate, probably worse because she'd kept this secret all along.

The door opened, and Jonatan returned with sandwiches and water. Behind him, through the open door, Bea caught a glimpse of the sky outside the library window. The sky looked so blue—so inviting.

He set a plate and glass in front of her before returning to the door to close it, cutting Bea off from the sky. He then pulled out the chair across from her to sit. Bea thought about what the woman said and wondered what would happen if Jonatan adjusted his theory.

"Do you remember when we first met and talked about Blake?"

Bea dabbed her mouth with a napkin. "We talked about *The Tyger* and *The Lamb*."

"That's right." He half smiled.

"I do remember that. I also remember that you didn't like what I had to say. You made me feel as though my thoughts were wrong. Invalid."

"I've been reflecting a lot on that conversation and how you concluded what the poem meant to you. While you are terribly wrong, I find it quite remarkable that you produced such a deeply thoughtful answer in the first place."

Bea narrowed her eyes at him.

"After what you have seen while working with me, do you still believe that God created the light and the darkness?"

"Yes."

"How can you possibly still believe that after all this time? How can you believe that God created a vile... creature such as that?" He gestured toward Emily.

Rage simmered beneath Bea's skin, twisting through her veins like wildfire. But she maintained her level-headedness as she challenged him. Bea was fully aware that she was about to step into dangerous territory. Yet, she needed Jonatan to understand how misguided and baseless his theory was. "Tell me, Jonatan, have you ever found that sin—that cancer—within any of the bodies you've autopsied?"

Jonatan slammed his hand on the table so hard that their dishes jumped and clattered. "You don't believe in what I am doing, do you?"

Bea stood her ground. "With those two poems of Blake's yes, that is exactly what I am saying. If God is so good and benevolent, why does he give certain people unfair lives of having to beg on the streets while others live like fat cats in their mansions? Why does God allow war and murder to happen? Why does God take away mothers from young daughters who are left with uncaring fathers—?"

She cut herself off from asking why men abduct women and force them into situations they don't want to be in. Bea knew she was right. She'd known all along. The polar dynamics of light and dark, good and evil, purity and sin have always coexisted in every being because God created it. And it all boiled down to the first human that ever existed.

"Jonatan, your research—"

He put his sandwich down. "What about my research?"

"What if the origin of sin you seek doesn't reside in women, but in men?"

His brows furrowed. "How dare you even suggest such a horrific idea? Women are the root of all evil. It was Eve who ate first from the Tree of Knowledge."

"She was coerced into doing it by the Devil. Who is a masculine figure!"

"How dare you!" He stood and slammed his hands on the table. "She had her own free will and knew God forbade eating of that tree."

He leaned in close to her. A feral fire reflected in his eyes.

In that moment, Bea realized Jonatan only considered her a friend as long as she didn't step outside his established parameters. Their friendship resembled a prison, akin to this room. He would never regard her as an equal or allow her to leave, containing her in these two small rooms forever.

Bea closed her eyes and remembered the brief glimpse of the outside just a few moments ago. *The sky looked so blue.*

"You're wrong," she said. "We don't choose to become fallen women! Selling ourselves is the life that men force us into. My father abused me, and I had to run away to survive. And the only way I would be able to make it was to se—"

Johnathon struck her.

Pain radiated through her face. Bea was briefly blinded as she was propelled out of her seat and landed face-first on the floor. Overhead, she heard Jonatan take three quick breaths.

"We?" he seethed. "WE? Have you been lying to me all this time?" He thrust a finger in Emily's direction. His face cracked with a mixed emotion of sadness and disbelief. "Are you one of them?"

Emily wasn't wrong. He would have found out, eventually. Jonatan wasn't her friend.

He seized her by her shoulder, his bony fingers digging into her thin flesh, and stood her to her feet. As Bea stepped backward to center her dizziness, he pushed her into the tray of surgical tools. The tray tipped, scattering the tools on the ground, with some of the scalpels lodged upright in the floorboards by their blades.

Bea stumbled but managed to catch herself before landing on top of them. Jonatan kicked her hard in the side, causing her to topple over and nearly land on his prized bistoury. The bistoury lay next to her right hand. She grabbed it by the handle and slid the sharpened side behind her back as she sat up.

Jonatan seized her by the shirt collar and pulled her up. With his face inches from hers, his hot breath, rank with salami and cheese, washed over her. "You're one of them, you whore. You've contaminated my research!" Jonatan started to shake Bea like a rag doll, and she tightened her grip on the bistoury's handle. "And now you'll end up just like them."

Bea knew another blow was coming. She whipped the bistoury out from behind her back, and, with all her strength, cut into his neck, right where he'd shown her—the left carotid artery.

Jonatan yelped and put a hand on the wound. Blood pulsed around his fingers. He staggered into the counter, then slid down against the cabinets to the floor. Bea was on him the moment he hit the floor, cutting the other side of his neck, bleeding him out.

Jonatan's mouth slackened. She watched the life fade from his eyes. When his hand fell away from his neck, his head drooped forward.

She grabbed him by the hair, held his head up, and cut across his throat, opening it wide, the blade connecting the cut carotid points, releasing his sinful breath. With his hair clutched in her hand, Bea pulled his head backward to further open the wound for the escaping air. And there, in that opening, she saw something out of place that she'd never seen inside the women's necks.

Bea bent Jonatan's head back, further expanding the opening to his neck cavity. With the tip of her finger, she probed inside the wound. Along the back of his esophagus was a massive greyish-white lump speckled in blood and mucus—a pearl hidden within the folds of an oyster.

"She was right," Bea whispered as she dropped the bistoury. "The cancer is inside men, not women." Digging the keys to her freedom out of Jonatan's breast pocket, Bea ran her hand down her leg and gripped the shackle. With a firm hold on the shackle key, she inserted it into the keyhole and turned. She freed herself.

"Thank you," Bea said to Emily as she pointed toward Jonatan's body. "You're correct. I found the sin in his throat."

Bea pulled Jonatan's apron off the hook. "It'll be good to have a woman to talk to from now on. Let's get you dressed."

She slipped the top loop of the apron over Emily's head. After a bit of maneuvering, she got the strings fastened around her waist. Bea struggled with Emily's body until she managed to wrap her arms under Emily's armpits and drag her off the table. Her feet hit the floor with a thud. Bea half-carried Emily over to a chair and set her upright. She slid the back of the chair against the wall to support Emily's head.

"There now. We've proven your theory once." Bea smiled. "But once isn't enough to be a scientific truth."

Bea stood tall. "But we cannot hide these results—cannot keep secrets within the walls of this house; no, we'll put the results out on display in town so that the folks there will know what we are trying to achieve. And they'll tell the world of our efforts."

A whoosh of relief escaped Bea's lungs as she felt a swell of life surge within her. She would no longer be a prisoner, but a contributor to society. She looked fondly at Emily. "Jonatan was wrong. Let us prove that sin doesn't reside within women but in men."

Bea picked the bistoury back up and wiped Jonatan's blood off the blade. Once cleaned, she held the glistening metal up to catch the light from the kerosene lamp hanging from the ceiling. The smile that spread across her face stretched from ear to ear. "I know a man who'll be the perfect specimen, as I'm sure he has more of this sinful disease inside of him than Jonatan."

Chapter 11

THIS IS HOW A VILLAIN IS MADE

"**B**EST TIME WE GET ready," Bea says to Emily as a dot appears on the horizon and grows larger as it moves steadily toward them along the road that cuts through the prairie. Bea stands up from the rocking chair and takes the teacups inside, placing them in the sink before returning to Emily's side. The cups can be washed later if there's time.

Bea lowers Emily's feet from the towel to the floorboards. Then she scoops up her friend's body and wobbles with Emily into the house, bumping into corners and walls along the way back to Jonatan's old office. The light from the front window filters in through the open door, casting a glow on her old chair, which is positioned against the closed closet door. She places Emily in the chair and runs her fingers through her friend's tangled hair.

"I need to find my brush later," Bea says, smoothing Emily's tresses and then untangling the stray hairs caught in her fingers. She readjusts the apron tied around Emily's neck and waist, covering her nudity. Unfortunately, it was the only article of clothing that Bea could muster to put on her friend by herself, especially given Emily's condition.

Emily's head tilts to the side as her cloudy eyes stare straight ahead. Bea adjusts Emily's arms to her sides, the feeling of mobility slightly returning to her friend's frame. A tear drips from Bea's eye as she kisses her friend's cheek. Since they worked on Jonatan, Emily has not said another word to Bea.

"Let's get ready," Bea says. She walks to the cabinet to fetch a box of matches and then returns to the table where she and Jonatan used to eat. She lights the match and lifts the globe off a kerosene lamp she brought from her old room, since she is too short to refill and relight the one on the ceiling. She never liked the placement of that lamp anyway, even though it provided more light.

Bea turns her attention to the autopsy table, where a white cloth—marked by a large, oval-shaped red stain—conceals whatever rests on the cold metal beneath. She slowly pulls the cloth back, its fabric clinging to the exposed flesh of the body.

Jonatan, mouth agape and eyes wide, stares at the ceiling. Bea refuses to close his eyes, as he must bear witness to their success. When she and Emily had performed a complete autopsy on Jonatan, they uncovered more than one specimen of sin within his body.

His neck is sliced horizontally at the throat, with a deep incision leading vertically down his torso to another horizontal split along his pubic line; Jonatan is flayed open, ribs cracked in two halves at the sternum. Internal organs and the white lumpy tissue of sin were removed—placed in two large jars left at the front door of Maggie's boarding house before sunrise this morning, alongside a note that said, "Sin and the missing women have been found." Bea scrawled Jonatan's name at the bottom of the note.

Bea pats the pockets of her pants, feeling the outline of the folded tortoise bistoury beneath the fabric. She's been carrying it on her ever since she picked it up yesterday.

"Doc!" a man's voice hollers from the front of the house.

"There's the sheriff. I'll go greet him," Bea tells Emily. She leaves the office without waiting for a reply, closing the door behind her but leaving it unlocked. As she walks into the library, the sheriff looms at the threshold of the front door.

"What's going on?" he leers at her.

"Hello, sir. What brings you here today?" Bea tries to maintain a neutral expression and not allow a smile to crack through.

"You. Why are you here?" the sheriff demands, stepping toward her. "Where is Jonatan?"

"In his office." She gestures to the hallway behind her. The sheriff leans to the right, peering over her shoulder into the house. "Would you like to come in?"

He looks at her, and a troubled expression flashes across his face before he regains his composure. "You're not supposed to be here."

Bea maintains the gentle expression, keeping her lips from revealing a smile. She steps back and slightly bows, her hand gesturing toward the office. "The doctor hired me on as his housekeeper. I've been here this whole time. Didn't you know?"

He rolls his lips between his teeth, and the fingertips of his right hand brush the hilt of the gun in its holster before he puts both hands on his hips. "Do you know about the message he left in town?"

Bea looks up at him. "I am not sure what you are talking about, but let's ask him."

"Probably best you wait here," the sheriff says. "It's business for men."

"Of course," she says. "I'll be in the kitchen."

"You stay occupied there while I speak with him." He crosses the threshold into the library. Bea feigns heading to the kitchen while listening to the sheriff march through the library toward the rear of the house. Quickly, she pivots to follow him, her bare feet silently gliding over the hardwood floor. She slips her hands into her pockets. The sheriff opens the door.

"What the hell!?" he shouts, hand on the doorknob and silhouetted by the light of the small kerosene lamp. Bea had left Jonatan exposed and in full view of whoever entered the room.

Bea pounces on the sheriff's back. Grabbing his left shoulder with her hand, she whips her right arm around his front, the blade of the opened bistoury catching the light. The metal touches his neck, and she depresses the blade against his flesh, separating the tissue as she draws the bistoury across his throat, letting his blood splatter across the floor to join the ghosts of yesterday's bloodstains from Jonatan.

There is a sick crackle as the sheriff exhales through the slit; his hands immediately go to his throat. He staggers backward into the hall, slamming Bea into the wall. They both fall to the ground. Bea wraps her arms and legs around him to pin him to her as he tries to flail. Hands smearing blood along the wall, fingers grasping at the air, grasping for her, but she holds him tight until his movements weaken. It isn't until he goes completely slack that she releases him.

Bea crawls out from underneath the body, covered in blood. She surveys the mess and sighs.

"What are we going to do with this?" she says, and looks at Emily, who is sitting in the same spot on the other side of the office. Bea sighs heavily. This is all just too much. She spent hours yesterday cleaning up the remnants of her research on Jonatan. And now she'll have to do the same for the sheriff.

The vile memory of the sheriff touching her—forcing her to touch him—flashes in her mind. Then, she thinks of Jonatan with his hands on Emily, fingers tightening around her neck. Emily's eyes wide and pleading as her hands beat against his shoulders and arms, trying to free herself. She can't. She can't.

A shudder tingles up Bea's spine, shaking her so much that she drops the bistoury into the pool of blood at her toes. Bea falls to her knees and lets out a wail, her small, shivering frame wracked with sobs.

"Emily!" she calls out, looking to her friend. "Emily!"

Jonatan had touched Emily, crushing her throat beneath his fingers and stealing her breath and her life. And what of the others? How many countless others had there been? Bea herself had lost track during her imprisonment in this room. Jonatan had convinced her that they were friends. But she was nothing more than a body existing within the confines of this small space to do his bidding. All the women like Emily were nothing more than specimens for Jonatan's own amusement. Nothing more.

A scream rips from her mouth, and she plants her hands firmly in the sheriff's blood, feeling the liquid warmth beneath her palms. Her screams continue as she looks to her friend—they are two broken, lost women. Bea no longer knows her place in life. The sheriff was riddled with sin—she didn't need to cut him open to know that. And she didn't need to prove that these vile men were full of it to the world. She knows. She and Emily *know*.

So many women lost at the hands of these men. And the world is so big. How many others are like Jonatan and the sheriff? Bea closes her mouth, ending the scream. She moves her hands left and right in the blood, smearing it on the floor. Sitting back on her haunches, she looks at Emily and holds up her blood-coated palms. "We didn't start out this way. This is how we were made!"

She wouldn't clean up this mess, as it has already been cleaned. Jonatan and the sheriff are gone. They will not harm another woman. Jonatan's research be damned.

But there are more—so many more like these two. Bea exhales and, using the hallway wall for support, stands up. The sheriff's body lies across the threshold of the office door, his blood seeping in all directions. Bea gazes at Emily, sitting proudly among the dead, like a queen at the head of the table, her lips hinting at the shadow of a smile.

"I love you, Emily," she says to her friend before picking up the bistoury. Taking it into the kitchen, she cleans the blood off it and her hands. Then she strips off the dirty clothes she's wearing to remove any blood that has seeped through the fabric onto her skin. Once her skin glistens, she dries the bistoury and folds it. She cares not for the watery crimson mess that now taints the sink area. Naked, she walks to the stairs and ascends. She heads to Jonatan's bedroom and then hesitates. The curtain around where she used to sleep was never taken down. She had forgotten to look for her belongings after she escaped Jonatan's office yesterday.

Her hand slips between the linens that section off her old room, and she sees her bag sitting in the center of the floor where her mattress used to be before it was moved to the closet in Jonatan's office. Her footprints leave a trail on the dusty floor as she walks over to her bag. Her fingertips lovingly slide across the wooden handle, and she pauses before opening it, fearing that nothing remains inside. The bag is the only item left in her possession from her past.

She unsnaps the handles and separates them. Inside is a pile of yellow fabric. Bea breathes in sharply; it's the same color as her mother's dress. Gingerly, she touches the fabric, feeling its familiar texture. Grasping it with both hands, she pulls it out to reveal her mother's dress. There's a faint discolored stain on the front from where she vomited when she first entered Jonatan's office, but overall, it appears to have been washed.

Another lie from Jonatan: he didn't get rid of it after all. Folding the dress in the crook of her left elbow, Bea looks inside the bag once more. Her other two dresses remain exactly as she left them, folded inside. Beneath them is her coin purse—the same one gifted by her mother all those years ago. She lifts it, surprised by its weight. Unclasping it, she discovers a folded stack of dollar notes. With shaky hands, Bea returns the money to the coin purse and closes it. She can't bring herself to count the money, but she knows it's more than what was originally there. Jonatan must have put what he owed her inside.

What could have led Jonatan to behave like this? A *fearful symmetry*. Jonatan embodied a paradox of moral ambiguity. Deep inside, he recognized that his actions were wrong, and to seek atonement, he tried to show care for Bea in his own disconcerting manner. He served as a prime example of not just man's sin but also of the disturbing coexistence of light and darkness within a single soul—a creature of duality created by God.

Bea takes her belongings to Jonatan's bedroom, slips on her mother's yellow dress, and relishes being back among its fabric. She combs her wild hair, and never once considers pinning it up—nor does she care about the fact that she's not wearing any undergarments.

She turns to Jonatan's dresser and rummages through the drawers; however, this time, she avoids the top drawer. The items in there belong to other women, not her. Nothing in that drawer is for her. Bea removes two sets of button-down shirts, slacks, and three pairs of socks from the remaining drawers, then places them in her bag. In the bottom drawer, she finds a cigar box full of money. Bea takes the box and returns to her bag to grab her coin purse.

She halves the money in her coin purse and adds it to the cigar box, then buries the cigar box under the clothes she took from the dresser. The coin purse is then placed in her left pocket. The bistoury knife goes into her right pocket, and she traces the outline of the instrument through the folds of the dress, savoring the comfort it brings to have it close at hand. In the washstand mirror, Bea finally allows herself to look at her reflection and doesn't recognize the woman looking back.

Her hair, once ending just below the bottom of her ribs, now trails down to her hips. She feels nothing when she thinks about how she truly doesn't know how long she has been imprisoned. A darkness haunts beneath her eyes, and there is a hollowness to her cheeks. For a moment, she thinks a different head is atop her body, but then laughs out loud at her silliness. This is who she is, and as Bea admires herself in the mirror for the first time since being locked away, she feels like a woman.

Bea discovers her old shoes in the back of Jonatan's closet. They are covered in dust. She uses his quilt to wipe them off. Unable to find her old stockings, she puts on a pair of Jonatan's socks. The shoes pinch as she squeezes her foot in. After struggling for a few moments, she takes off the socks and slides her bare feet in. The shoes remain tight, squeezing her toes together. How on earth did she manage with shoes before?

"These are ghastly contraptions!" she says, as she buttons them closed. "I'll have to get new ones in Denver City. Shoes with a little more room."

She stands, her ankles unsteady in the unfamiliar heels. "We've handled worse than sore feet," she grumbles. After taking one last look in the mirror, she smiles.

With her bag in hand, Bea makes her way downstairs. She sets her bag next to the front door and returns to the office. The sticky scent of the sheriff's blood hangs heavily in the air. Bea gingerly walks into the room, careful to step around the pooled blood. She averts her eyes from the sheriff and Jonatan's bodies to look at the notebooks spread across the counter, filled with Jonatan's ramblings and confessions of sin—wrongly misplaced and misguided. He was so naïve.

She never read what he had written in his own note-books, respecting his privacy. A weight of disgust hangs heavily on her shoulders, extinguishing any burning desire to read about what he'd written when he first considered her as his control in his research.

Grabbing a handful of pages, she rips them from the notebook's binding and scatters them around the room. Bea repeats this action with the textbooks that remain in the room. Piles of paper soon litter the office, with some pages starting to soak up the sheriff's blood. Bea walks over to Emily and gently places a hand on her cheek.

"Thank you for helping me find my way. I'll never forget you, my friend." She kisses Emily on the cheek once more before smoothing her hair. Bea turns to the table and picks up the burning kerosene lamp, carrying it out of the office.

Once over the threshold, she turns and hurls the lamp across the room, crashing it into the door that leads to the closet—her old room. The glass shatters. Bursting flames rain down on the scattered papers and wooden floor. The room instantly ignites. Bea picks up her bag and turns her back on the inferno. A warm breeze coils through the open door, wrapping around her like a promise. Without looking back, Bea steps into the sunlit unknown, leaving behind the ashes of who she used to be.

Acknowledgements

This book would not exist without the unwavering encouragement of Mary SanGiovanni, Maurice Broaddus, Norman Prentiss, Jeff Strand, and John Urbancik. *This is How a Villain is Made* began as a short story called *The Sky Looked So Blue* and was submitted to the March 2023 Scares That Care Writers Bootcamp. Their feedback was immediate and resounding: Bea had more to say—much more. She demanded space. She demanded a voice.

I spent the rest of 2023 writing her story. It was a raw, intense, and often brutal journey. There were nights I stared down the ghosts of my past—recalling relationships marked by narcissism, manipulation, and control—to find the words that would do Bea justice.

Thank you to Quinn at Quill & Bone Editing, who encouraged me with feedback that showed me I could push my limits and explore those dark places. I also sincerely thank Candace Nola of Uncomfortably Dark for recognizing the significance of this story. I also appreciate her guidance on how to handle certain scenes in Bea's story that I found extremely challenging to write as an ACE individual.

At the time of this book's release, the United States faces a political and social climate seemingly intent on clawing back hard-won freedoms, especially those of women and the LGBTQIA+ community. As I edited the final draft of this manuscript in early 2025, a growing sense of dread settled over me, as if decades of progress unraveled. But alongside that fear, something more intense grew—rage. Not quiet. Not demure. Unbridled, unapologetic rage that refuses to be silenced or softened for anyone's comfort. Bea's story, though fictional, resonates with truth, high-lighting resilience and a fierce reminder that no matter the trials, we always rise and never look back.

We will not be contained.

We are in our villain era.

About the Author

Amanda Headlee

Amanda Headlee is the author of *Till We Become Monsters, Madness and Greatness Can Share the Same Face, This is How a Villain is Made*, and several short stories. A devoted connoisseur of cosmic and psychological horror, she is often found unraveling the universe's darkest secrets—preferably with a steaming cup of chai tea in hand.

As a wandering wonderer, Amanda spends her free time riding one of her many bikes or hiking the Appalachian Mountains. She shares her Pennsylvania abode with a plethora of exotic plants and a horror-loving pup named Sprout.

You can follow Amanda on Facebook, Instagram, Twitter, and her website.

Website: www.amandaheadlee.com
BlueSky: @amandaheadlee.bsky.social
Instagram/Threads: @amandaheadlee
Facebook: @authorAmandaHeadlee